Also by Jan Springer

A Hero Escapes
A Hero Betrayed
A Hero's Kiss
A Hero Wanted
Captive Heroes

Pleasure Bound Boxed Set
Pleasure Bound : COMPLETE SERIES SciFi Erotic Romance Boxed
Set

Tentacles Shifter Erotic Romance
Taken by Him

The Key Club
A Merry Menage Christmas
Sophie's Menage
Jewel's Menage
Jaxie's Menage
A Homecoming Menage Christmas

The Outlaw Lovers
Jude
The Claiming
Colter's Revenge
Tyler's Woman
Resistance

The Outlaw Lovers
Alpha Outlaws Boxed Set

Vampira
Sweet Heat
Wet Heat
Crimson Heat

Standalone
A Touch of Menage Boxed Set
Shades of Menage Boxed Set
Naughty Girl Desires Boxed Set
Nice Girl Naughty
Sinderella Sexy
The Biker and The Bride
The Fire Within
Bared to Him
Pleasure Bound : A Futuristic Adult Romance Boxed Set
Merry Menage Kisses Boxed Set
Stripped Naked
Risqué Girl Delights Boxed Set
A Holiday Menage
Ménage À Trois
A Hitman for Hannah
Billionaire Boyfriend

Watch for more at www.janspringer.com.

A Holiday Ménage

Jan Springer

When the local swingers' club throws a Ménage Night Before Xmas party for charity, Roxie learns that scrumptious blue-collar worker Evan Johnston will be playing doctor...

Evan is playing doctor and he wants a certain special fantasy lady to be his Christmas Eve patient...he's also offering her an erotic sensual exam—along with a sizzling ménage e trois.

Roxie is desperate to be Evan's patient. Dressed in a Santa hat, red latex body suit and a cute pair of mistletoe earrings, she knows there's no better way to intimately get to know the guy who's stolen her heart than by stealing some sexy kisses under the mistletoe and hopping on the gyno table for the hottest physical of her life.

Please note: A Holiday Menage was previously published as Let's Get Physical by another publisher.

Published by Spunky Girl Publishing
Copyright 2016 by Jan Springer
Edited by Megyn Ashley
Discover other titles by Jan Springer at http:www.janspringer.com[1]

Notes

Trademarks Acknowledgement

The author acknowledges the trademarked status and trademark owners of the following wordmarks mentioned in this work of fiction:

GM: General Motors Corporation

Styrofoam: Dow Chemical Company

Chapter One

Roxie's breath slammed up in her lungs and every nerve ending in her body hummed to life as she watched Evan Johnston coming toward her. He was naked. Totally, utterly naked, except for the cute red and white Santa Claus hat he wore and the doctor's stethoscope hanging around his neck. He grinned with wicked intent and happiness bubbled inside her. How had she managed to grab the sexiest guy in the RV factory where they both worked? Gosh, this had to be some hot naughty dream. Evan wouldn't want a plain girl like her, would he?

Why not? An inner voice cheered. *You may not be a beauty queen but you aren't a total ugly duckling either.*

Evan's body looked tense as he studied her. His erection was hard and thick and very long. The bunched muscles in his wide chest and right arm jerked wonderfully as he stroked his engorged shaft. He touched himself with steady strokes as he studied her with the darkest, brownest eyes she'd ever seen.

"I've waited a long time for this, Roxie," he whispered as he lowered himself onto the bed beside her. His body heat splashed around her in hot waves and his musky scent destroyed her senses.

The mattress moved beneath Roxie as Evan stretched out and then turned to face her, his hand stroking and touching. He was doing to his cock what she wanted to do him. But she couldn't touch him because her wrists were bound. Her arms were stretched out over her head, tied to the headboard with green silk stockings. Her legs were spread, her ankles bound.

She loved this helpless feeling. Loved the wicked way he looked at her. Knew she was totally at his mercy.

"I've wanted you too. So badly," she breathed harshly.

"So why didn't you ever tell me, sweetness? Couldn't you tell how much I wanted to be with you?" He looked down and she followed his gaze to where he continued touching himself.

Have mercy, but he just kept growing, didn't he? A web of pulsing veins laced his red flushed shaft and his plum-shaped cock head was turning an angry, demanding shade of purple. His sac was so swollen she wouldn't be surprised if he ached like crazy. Her pussy clenched on empty air as she willed him to enter her.

"I know you want me to make love to you. You want me to take you fast and ride you hard. To give you what we've both denied ourselves for so long. But first, a kiss."

He leaned over her, his free hand, large and calloused from his job as a maintenance man, splayed out on her lower abdomen like a fire brand. He lowered his head and his warm mouth covered hers, short-circuiting her thoughts. His lips stroked hers, his tongue slid into her with one demanding push that had her whimpering at his forcefulness. She was helpless beneath an onslaught of sensations as his tongue stroked into her like a mini cock.

The hand on her belly moved down to between her open thighs. She moaned into his mouth as a finger pressed between her labia and entered her wet vagina.

"You're flooding down here, sweetness," he groaned in a low and husky voice.

Evan's withdrew his finger and using her sticky wetness, he circled her clit, slowly, torturously. Tension raged through her. He slipped his finger into her again, collecting more juices then massaging her sensitive clit. To and fro, he slid his finger until she was clenching her thighs and aching for him to take her. Her hips instinctively arched, exposing her pussy. She craved him, needed him.

She wanted to tighten her thighs, but the binds prevented it. She wanted to grab his cock and bring him into her, but she couldn't. Frustration mingled with arousal and she moaned louder, the desperation pulsing through her as her desires quickly reached toward the out-of-control boundary. The boundary she rarely crossed unless she knew someone. Trusted someone. Could she do it for Evan, a virtual stranger?

"Come for me, sweetness," he purred against her mouth as he broke the kiss. His breaths were hot against her face. Her body ached for him. Craved him. Her blood rushed through her veins like white-hot lightning and her vagina gripped his finger as he came in for more lube.

He put more pressure on her clit as he swept over it with quickening speed. Her breaths were ragged and irregular. She licked his lower lip as he kissed the edge of her mouth. So sweetly. She trembled against him. Loved the featherlight kisses. Enjoyed the thrust of his finger as he slid over her clit and pistoned into her vagina.

"I'm getting really hard for you, Roxie. Really hard. But first I want you to come for me. Come for me." His voice sounded tortured.

Her heart thundered in her chest. Perspiration blossomed over her forehead. She fought the binds. Wanted to touch him. Wanted to control his cock. To bring him into her. But she was helpless.

"Evan? Please? Cut me loose," she whispered. Desperation slashed through her. She wanted him to untie her. She wanted to take control. She was so hot. Her body on fire now as two fingers plunged into her vagina. Then three.

She could hear the suctioning sound as her wetness welcomed him in with every thrust. Could feel her body bucking, tightening. Tensing.

And then she was exploding. Crying out as he withdrew his fingers and came over her. His thick, hard cock impaling her in one brutally beautiful thrust that had her gasping. His mouth covered hers again, his lips desperately sliding over hers and he was thrusting in and out and she accepted the blistering waves as he rode her hard. So damn hard. Yes! Oh God yes...

"Roxie! Come on! The Medical Fetish bidding is going to start any minute and we've got to get you ready for your intimate physical!" Thirty-year-old Roxie Whitney's friend, Gina, shouted above the pounding Christmas rock music as she rushed off the dance floor.

Actually Gina was the one who was late, for Pete's sakes. Roxie had been waiting, her insides a ball of nervous excitement, as she stood like a Christmas wallflower at the edge of the dance floor. She'd been watching Gina writhe like a wild woman amidst the crush of bodies in her crisp black, tight gothic nurse's uniform with thigh high, black fish net stockings and five-inch heels. Her nervousness was why she'd turned to her fantasies. Of Evan.

Gosh, she'd gotten so into that fantasy she was literally drenched between her thighs and feeling a wee bit flushed.

Oh why couldn't she be more like Gina? She would have had Evan in her bed before now.

Her roommate, coworker at the plant and good friend Gina.

Pretty. Popular. Adventurous. Not afraid to dance. But Roxie was the total opposite. That's what had attracted her to Gina in the first place. The woman was unafraid of anything.

Before Roxie could set her friend straight on who was waiting for whom, Gina grabbed her by the hand and pulled her into the throng of swingers and then through a door, up the narrow staircase overflowing with poinsettias and garland to the second floor where the change rooms were located.

"You are going to love what I picked up for you." Gina grinned, her dark brown Italian eyes glittering with mischief as she unlocked her locker with her key.

A huge shot of nervousness grabbed hold of Roxie and suddenly what had seemed like an exciting idea in allowing Gina to dress her for the Medical Night Before Xmas swinger's party didn't seem like such a good idea anymore. Suddenly it seemed rather scary to put her trust into such a bold and daring woman like Gina.

"This is what I got for you, hon. You are going to stand out from everybody else, catch Evan's eye and he is going to be panting all over you and wanting to get into your pants when he sees you in it."

Yes, another reason she liked Gina. She got straight to the point.

From the locker Gina withdrew a blood red latex jumpsuit with black buckle belt and sexy four-inch heeled sandals. Roxie's mouth dropped open in shock. First of all it was medical fetish night not latex rubber night and second of all, would this outfit even fit her? It looked as if it had been made for someone...skinny, and thin she was not.

"I knew you'd like it." Gina winked and held the garment up against Roxie. "Here, hold it. You are going to look so hot; Evan is going to self-combust. Here's a sexy Santa Claus hat to go with it and cute little mistletoe earrings." Gina plopped the green jewelry that truly did look like little balls of mistletoe dangled from small gold hoops, a felt red hat with a bunch of white fluff around the trim and a huge white pom pom on the top of the hat onto a nearby bench.

"Meet me downstairs when you're ready."

Before Roxie could ask Gina to hang around, mainly because she was a shy chickenshit to be seen in this outfit, Gina had fled the change room as if her ass itself were on fire.

Shit! Roxie swore as she turned her attention to the smooth red suit and her heart beat like a drummer boy beating his drum.

What had she gotten herself into?

* * * * *

Thirty-five-year-old Evan Johnston began searching for the woman of his sexual fantasies the instant he entered the swinger's club. Rumor had it Roxie would be here tonight and Evan wanted to make sure rumor was fact because if she wasn't here he'd just hightail back to his solitary farmhouse before tonight's forecasted snowstorm hit and start his Christmas vacation snuggled up to his three feline companions and two golden retrievers.

Despite the impending bad weather, the swinger's club was packed. The owners had outdone themselves with the Christmas decorations. Pristine miniature buttery yellow twinkling lights were strung in zigzag motion across the ceiling of the dance floor. Large, frosty blue and white Styrofoam snowflakes dangled between the strings giving the ceiling a snowstorm effect. Quite fitting for what was supposed to be coming later.

He couldn't believe he was here tonight. Normally, he'd be back in his hometown of Oshawa, Ontario with family over the holidays but this year he'd opted to hang around here, small town Solitary, Alberta, a few short miles outside of Calgary, so he could catch Roxie.

He still remembered the first time he'd seen her at work. He'd been hit hard and he'd known he had the family curse. His dad had warned him it would happen. Dad should know, the curse had struck him as well as his brother and then his sister. Now it was his turn. He'd been trying to deny it for weeks now, but every time he thought of Roxie, his heart raced, his palms sweat and he could barely form a thought unless it involved her.

The few times he'd run into his sudden object of infatuation, they'd been at work. He'd started at the RV plant several weeks ago and he noticed she appeared shy and nervous, darting him interested glances but not being bold about her interest in him. He liked that shyness about her. She was a refreshing change from some of the more adventurous women he'd dated in the past. One thing that surprised him was that Roxie was a swinger and frequented this club. He wasn't sure if this latest tidbit was a good thing or not. Good in his fantasy world, because every time he showered and every night he went to bed, he masturbated to her vision. In reality though, would she be interested in him? A guy with limited experience in the swinger's scene?

Just then he spotted his good friend and coworker Brody Cohen, making his way through the throng of people toward Evan.

"Hey, man, glad you could make it." Brody gave Evan a high five in greeting and the two of them headed for the room where the bidding would take place.

"Feeding the animals took a bit longer than I expected," Evan admitted as he and Brody signed their names to the list of people who would be playing doctor and bidding on a patient.

"You need a wife to help you with that old hobby farm you bought." Brody grinned, showing off a nice set of white teeth against his deeply tanned face. Evan suspected his friend did the tanning booth thing to keep such an even color due to the fact it was dark when they got to work and dark when they got off.

"When I get a wife, she won't be feeding the animals, she'll be feeding me." Evan laughed and stepped into the large room, which was already half full with bidders, patient wannabes and onlookers. Toward the back of the room a sea of mostly white wavered. Obviously that's where the doctors and nurses had congregated. Many were dressed up in the traditional pristine white lab coats, wearing stethoscopes and name tags, while others playing nurses wore tight uniforms of varying colors and Florence Nightingale style nurse's caps with red crosses blazed across the front.

Most of the patients were dressed in casual clothes, some were in the Christmas spirit decked out in green elf suits or Santa Claus and some wore stuffed reindeer antlers. Not that they would need their outfits once they were herded into their respective examination rooms and instructed to undress for their intimate physical exams for their respective play doctors.

Word had it Roxie wanted to experience a threesome here tonight and she was going to be a patient up for bid. Evan and Brody had already agreed to pool their money to bid on her as a dual doctor team.

Tonight's Medical Night Before Xmas fetish party was for charity, all proceeds going to a local homeless shelter. And if they played their money right Evan would be getting his fantasy woman in the stirrups of a gynecological table. The thought of her naked and her thighs spread wide open for the two of them, made Evan almost moan as his cock throbbed and swelled hard against his jeans.

Instead of wearing a lab coat like many of the others were wearing, he'd opted for pale blue scrub pants and top with a loose mask and stethoscope dangling around his neck as if he were just coming out of an operating room. Brody wore a short sleeved Dr. Kildare style lab jacket with the words Dr. Kildare emblazoned on the breast pocket.

Brody admitted he was really into the medical scene and knew all the fun items that this swinger's club offered their clients. His exotic stories of how arousing it was to physically examine a woman on a gyno table and that Roxie would be here up for grabs tonight were what had encouraged Evan to step out of his comfort zone. He usually spent a quiet evening back at the farmhouse tending his animals and heading into the shower to masturbate while fantasizing about one cute as sin woman named Roxie Whitney.

Man, every time he thought about her, his heart fluttered stupidly. He liked her wispy shoulder-length brown hair and the way she parted it to one side and let her bangs feather across her forehead. And her sparkling green eyes did a nice number on his insides too.

She was tall. Almost six feet, he guessed. Tall women like that were rare for him. She actually had some meat on her bones. She obviously had a good appetite and her cheeks always seemed to glow a nice rosy shade. But the best thing he liked about her was her pink, cupid-bow shaped lips. Very sweet looking and kissable.

His gut twisted in that odd, neat way it always did when he thought about how tenderly he would kiss her. His lips would press firmly against hers so she would know he meant business and wanted to claim her as his own. And her succulent mouth would open and let him inside and—

A painful nudge to his gut from Brody snapped Evan back to reality. Brody nodded toward the entrance where Gina, Roxie's roommate, not to mention Brody's ex-wife, was dolled up in a black nurse's uniform and signing one of the sheets indicating she would be participating tonight also.

"So where's Roxie?" Evan asked when he didn't see her.

"Why don't we ask Gina?" Brody smiled and started toward his ex-wife.

A weird kind of disappointment shifted through Evan at not seeing Roxie yet and suddenly he wasn't so sure he wanted to know if Roxie had decided not to show.

Chapter Two

Roxie stared in shock at her reflection in the full-length mirror. Was this woman who stared back at her really her?

The red latex suit fit her like a glove, illuminating her curves, accenting her wide hips and making her waist look smaller than it really was. And with the Santa Claus hat plopped on her head and the dangling mistletoe earrings she looked Christmasy and sexy all rolled into one. Gina sure did know her stuff. She was right too. With most patients wearing regular clothing, she certainly would be an eye catcher.

Gosh, she could barely recognize herself.

Early this morning she'd gone to the salon and they'd put auburn streaks through her otherwise mousey-colored hair. The highlights gave her hair much needed life. Her green eyes, what she considered her best asset, seemed an even deeper shade of green because she'd splashed on some emerald eye shadow. With some concealing makeup, she'd managed to make her slightly too wide nose look narrower at the bridge and what she liked to call her Marilyn Monroe mole on her upper left lip now looked a bit darker after dabbing it with a dark makeover pen.

Yep, she definitely looked hot on the outside. Inside, however, was a different story. Inside, she wanted to run and grab her favorite pair of jeans and loose fitting top and just hang out and watch Gina dance away on the dance floor. It was fun watching her friend operate her men and when Gina grabbed one or two and headed to one of the swinger's sex rooms, Roxie would sometimes pick up a guy who wanted some fast sex or take off and go to a movie by herself before coming home and cuddling up in bed with her two fat cats.

Not tonight, an inner voice warned.

Tonight, you are going to catch that man of your dreams and reel him into your vagina.

She creamed at the thought and shivered as excitement splashed around her latex covered body. Yes, Gina was right. If Roxie was ever going to break out of her shell and grab Evan's attention, this outfit would do it. Taking a few deep breaths for some much needed courage, Roxie headed out the change room door.

* * * * *

"Where's Roxie?" Brody asked.

Gina ignored Brody and her dark brown eyes twinkled knowingly as she gazed past her ex and fixed Evan with a hot stare, which made him feel like a butterfly being pinned to a board by a butterfly collector.

"Who wants to know? Brody? Or you?" she asked as she held Evan's gaze. He'd met Gina at work on several occasions. She seemed pretty nice and not shy at all so wasn't surprised at her bold question.

"Hey, I can't help it if my new friend here is a little shy." Brody laughed as he slapped Evan on his back a little too hard. Obviously Brody felt tense at having his ex-wife here at the swinger's club. From what Evan had heard through the rumor mill it was Gina's need to explore her sexuality with other men and other women outside of their bedroom that was one of the main reasons the two divorced. But Brody never spoke of it and Evan never asked.

"So? Where is she?" Brody prodded.

"She's around here somewhere."

Evan sighed in relief. Yes, Roxie was here. The plan to get her on a gyno table would hopefully go off without a hitch.

Gina smiled and reached out to smooth away a wrinkle on Brody's white lab coat.

"I'm guessing you're playing a young Dr. Kildare tonight, Brody? I'm playing doctor tonight too with a female patient. Maybe next time you can play patient and I'll pick you up?" Gina drawled as she scratched a set of long black-painted nails along Brody's forearm, leaving a nice trail of red-colored flesh.

"I'm always the doctor, sweetheart. Never the patient," Brody chirped in a little bit higher voice than usual, leading Evan to think Brody's ex was definitely having an effect on him.

Gina retracted her claws and smiled warmly at Brody.

"Tis a shame. I'm never the patient either, remember? I prefer to be the one on top and in charge. Always. So I guess we'll never get the chance to give each other intimate physicals. I so looked forward to getting your cock nice and hard and giving it some tender loving care."

She pursed her succulent black lips at Brody, indicating oral sex and Evan watched Brody's Adam's apple bob up and down frantically.

Just then a round of catcalls split the air, and from the corner of his eye Evan spied a splash of red. He turned to see who was causing the commotion and blinked in stunned disbelief when he saw her.

Roxie.

His Roxie.

Holy shit.

Now it was his turn to be at a loss for words as he watched the red foxy lady sign her name on one of the participating sheets before entering the room. Clad in one mother of a tight latex suit and Santa hat, she literally took his breath away.

She looked awesome. More than awesome. He hadn't known she had so many nice curves. Very nice.

His cock and balls certainly did agree as they quickly swelled and throbbed with intense need.

"Play nice with her boys. She's a back door virgin," Gina cooed, then left them, heading toward Roxie.

"Holy...shit," Brody mumbled, echoing Evan's earlier reaction to first seeing Roxie.

Evan shot Brody a curious look and relaxed as Brody's eyes remained glued to Gina's swinging backside. She wore a very tight and very short black skirt which gave a nice eyeful of long legs and the bottom curves of a luscious shaped ass.

"So, go after her. Tell her you'll be her patient tonight."

Brody smiled wryly, as if knowing some sort of secret.

"No way. If Gina wants me, she'll have to break. I am man. She is woman. Man never submits to woman. She seems to have forgotten that's why we divorced. Besides I like the wait. Gina will submit. Eventually. It won't be tonight. Maybe not for a long time. But I'll let her live out her fantasies. Then when she's ready I'll be making her pay big time when she climbs back into my bed. Now that chick in red over there," he nodded to Roxie, breaking off the subject of Gina, "looks like every male and some females in here want her for their patient. We may have a battle on our hands. I bet Gina had a hand in this. Dressing up Roxie so we have to pay through the nose to get her. Bitch-ex must be jealous. Not half as much as I am when I see her with some other...guy." Brody let the words trail off but Evan didn't say anything. Obviously Brody and his ex still had a load of shit to deal with, but that wasn't going to stop Evan from giving Roxie her ménage fantasy tonight.

Roxie turned her head and met Evan's gaze. He read surprise at seeing him here and then that nervous excitement that buzzed around her gorgeous green eyes whenever she looked at him. Jolts of lightning ripped through his body and Evan had to inhale slowly to steady his suddenly increasing heartbeat.

Just looking at her made him feel so hot.

"You're mine," he mouthed to her and enjoyed her returning timid smile.

"Come on, the bidding is about to begin," Brody urged and they headed to the standing area at the back of the room to watch as the patients were presented to the bidders.

The front of the room had a makeshift stage and a bit of a runway for the patients to model themselves. Evan and Brody watched as one after the other, patients were paraded, inspected and ultimately sold off to the doctors. Beside him, Brody tensed as Gina nabbed herself a gorgeous tall, svelte black woman who wore a collar and chain. As Gina led her patient past them, she winked at Brody, who said nothing. But Evan didn't miss the muscles in his friend's jaw clench with frustration.

Finally Roxie appeared on the stage and Evan's heart once again began a mad thump.

"Bidding starts at fifty dollars! Do I hear fifty for Miss Santa Seductress?"

"Fifty!" Evan and several others shouted at the same time.

Damn eager beavers. Evan glared at one or two of them as they stared at him. He didn't recognize any of them from work, or he would have gone over and slipped them some bribe money so they wouldn't bid.

He watched Roxie move like a goddess as she strolled along the stage. Her sweet hips swayed and he ached to curl his hands around her waist, hold her steady and impale her pussy. His cock throbbed and hurt blossomed up his shaft and into his balls.

Oh man. He should have asked her out on a simple date instead.

Roxie's heart pounded at a major speed every time she caught Evan's gaze. She couldn't believe so many people were bidding for her. Even women! But most had dropped away as the price to purchase her for the evening continued to grow higher. The room had crowded to bursting as more and more onlookers gathered to watch. But Roxie made herself oblivious to them. As far as she was concerned only Evan existed in the room. He looked so handsome in his blue scrubs with a stethoscope and mask hanging around his neck. Just like a real McDreamy doctor. And Brody looked pretty sharp himself decked out in his Dr. Kildare garb.

The bidding was now between Evan and Brody's team and two bald men. Big bald men that looked like cuddly teddy bears. She'd seen the men dancing with Gina earlier tonight. The three appeared to have hit it off, laughing together and giggling as if they were old friends. That was another thing she liked about Gina. She made friends easily. Within minutes of meeting her, Roxie felt as if Gina were an old treasured friend and someone she'd known all her life.

But Roxie couldn't seem to trust anyone easily. Maybe it had something to do with her parents splitting up when she was five. Her mom had taken her but then she'd remarried almost immediately and had a couple more kids and Roxie had been cast aside. At least that's the way she'd felt. She'd withdrawn. At the age of eight she'd been sent to live with her dad and his new family. She'd felt the same there. An outsider. An intruder. So, she'd found solace in a world of books, tuning everybody out and everybody had pretty much left her alone. By her teenage years, she hadn't developed any social skills to help her associate with other kids her age, so she'd just been a loner. Eventually she'd become accustomed to her life being that way.

That is, until she'd met up with Gina last year. They shared the same apartment building and Gina had just divorced Brody. The cheerful woman had taken Roxie under her wing and they'd moved in with each other to help save their money. It was the first time since she'd been a kid that she felt as if she could open up with someone. She'd even helped Gina get a job at the plant where Roxie had worked since graduating high school.

Then several weeks ago she'd seen Evan pushing that mop on his first day of work. Something inside her had suddenly longed to go up to him and introduce herself. He was the new guy and like always when a new guy, or girl for that matter, started at the plant, everyone buzzed around them. Evan seemed popular. Gina said he was easy going and joked with the women easily, deflecting their questions about whether he was attached or dating someone serious.

One night when Gina was on a rare night at home, Roxie confided her frustrations about wanting to get to know Evan a bit more, but her fear of relationships stood in her way. That's when Gina suggested Roxie meet Evan at the swinger's club both Gina and herself frequented. And that she'd heard Evan and Brody were participating as duo doctors in the Club's Medical Night Before Xmas charity event.

Something unbelievably wicked and delightful unleashed inside Roxie at the thought of having no strings sex with both men. She could just give them control. They could do with her whatever they wished while she lay on a gynecological table spread bare for them.

And as Gina suggested, no-strings sex was one way to find out if Evan was any good in bed. No need for awkward dating. Sex was all that mattered in the end—that was Gina's motto.

And so with a little more prodding from Gina, Roxie had agreed to come here tonight as a patient in the hopes Brody and Evan would bid on her. Now she stood here, wearing this latex suit, a fever of excitement whipping through her and a butt plug stuffed up her ass.

"Two hundred!" Evan's confident voice zipped through Roxie, snapping her back to the present. Two hundred? Was Evan crazy? No one had bid that high on previous patients.

The bald guys both cursed softly and quickly conversed with each other.

Roxie held her breath. Could the bidding finally be over? Would the bald guys concede?

Despite their big sizes, the baldies seemed more like huge cuddly teddy bears with endearing smiles. She probably would have enjoyed having sex with them for her very first ménage, but she had her heart set on Evan and Brody.

The words "Sold! To Dr. Evan and Dr. Brody!" slashed through the tension filled air.

"Miss Santa Seductress, please follow your doctors to physical exam room number nine!" the barker bellowed over the cheers.

Oh my God! She was about to experience her first ménage è trois! And with Evan!

Roxie could barely walk through the throng of well wishers to where Brody and Evan waited for her near the door.

"I told you that you were mine," Evan said in a deep confident whisper.

Brody winked in greeting.

"I'll lead the way," he said and maneuvered himself in front of them, moving them through the crush of bodies who had come to watch the bidding.

Roxie shivered with excitement and a good shot of nervousness when Evan's hand branded across her lower back as he led her after Brody.

Chapter Three

"You're fully prepared?" he asked in a low voice so only she could hear as they walked down the hallway.

She nodded numbly. She knew what he meant. Fully prepared as in butt plug and birth control.

"Good. We doctors will give you an intimate exam you won't be forgetting any time soon."

Roxie's breath hitched at his comment.

Just as Brody disappeared into the room, Evan's hand against Roxie's back shifted to the left side of her waist. Before Roxie knew what was happening he'd moved her in such an erotic and easy way against the wall, her back pressing against the cold, hard concrete that she could only blink in stunned surprise at him. His face was mere inches from hers and his warm breath caressed her cheeks.

"Are you sure about this, sweetness?" he asked forcefully, a hand lifting to caress the side of her chin in such an intimate, gentle touch that she almost moaned out loud at how good it felt.

His question surprised her. Did she look *that* nervous? "Why do you ask? I wouldn't have signed up if I wasn't serious." *About you*, she added silently.

His eyes glittered with satisfaction and sexual intent.

"You don't seem the type to be a swinger. You're all shy and nervous around me," he said softly.

Not the type? Inwardly she smiled.

"What type do you think I am?" she breathed, deflecting the shy and nervous comment. He didn't need to know she reacted to him that way because he was the first guy she'd every really liked at first sight.

"I mean, you did bid on me, so you had something naughty in mind, didn't you?" If he had been serious, would he not just have asked her out on a date or for coffee? He'd had ample opportunity at work.

The corners of his luscious lips quirked upward ever so slightly. That tiny smile made her heart suspend in her chest.

God, was she pathetic or what? Getting all sweet on a man who only wanted to fuck her tonight and be on his way when he was satisfied.

But this is what you want too, Roxie, remember?

No strings sex. No dating. Just raw primal sex with the swingers. Love him and leave him. *Screw him before he screws you just like pretty much everybody in your life has done up until now.*

Roxie blinked in shock at that realization. She'd never really thought of it that way. At least not in depth. She'd made it a point from early on not to feel sorry for herself, so why start now?

"Well, if your trembling is an indication, I'd say you don't do this ménage thing very often."

She shook her head. "You two are my first."

Intense desire flared in his eyes and his head lowered. She trembled harder. Funny thing was she had no idea why she was shaking like a leaf.

"You do realize you leave me no choice but to kiss you...mistletoe on your earrings and all," he whispered and his hot mouth smoothed over hers, confident, forceful and with wicked possession.

Heat poured through her.

You're mine. Isn't that what he'd mouthed earlier? If the strong way his lips spread over hers was an indication, he certainly meant it.

Her thoughts scattered as his kiss deepened. He tasted good, she realized, after she grew accustomed to the initial shock of the erotic burn sweeping through her body. His lips were hot and smooth and wonderful sensations raced through her bloodstream making her breasts swell, her nipples harden and her pussy cream warmly.

His hands cupped her ass and as he kissed her harder, he massaged her butt cheeks so perfectly, she moaned softly into his mouth. His lips stroked hers, his tongue boldly pressing into her mouth and smoothing against her teeth. She knew he wanted her to part her teeth and let him in further. But she wasn't ready to trust him with that just yet. She rarely let a guy she didn't know into her mouth. It just seemed too intimate. Thankfully he backed off, realizing her hesitation.

The firmness of his kiss made her tipsy, as if she was sweetly drunk. Lifting her hands, she settled them on his hips. Firm, hot flesh flamed through his scrubs and scalded her fingertips.

He took her mouth deeply, his tongue stealing away any self-control she had as he licked her lips and those sweet, unexplained trembles shimmering through her ebbed away, changing into something sensual and alluring.

Instinctively she pressed against him, feeling his swollen erection. Encouraged by her movements, he swept against her too, his large cock head pressing into her lower belly.

Oh wow, he was built down there. Nice and big.

A driving ache deep inside her vagina urged her to take his cock into her hands and bring his flesh into her. But his kiss kept most of her attention away from what was happening through her body. She grew hotter. Perspiration dotted her forehead and popped out between her breasts.

He kissed her deeper, his hands leaving her ass, sliding up her belly to cover her breasts. He squeezed her mounds gently as if testing their fullness. Arousal rocked her. She moaned. It was a deep guttural animalistic sound she'd never heard before. She fought for air and he finally stopped the kiss.

"Now that was really nice," he whispered against her ear, taking her ear lobe into his volcanic mouth. He sucked so sweetly she shuddered. He dropped his hands from her breasts and acting casually, as if nothing had just happened between them, he took her hand and led her into the examination room on her weakened knees.

"Everything ready?" Evan asked as they entered.

"All prepared," Brody replied as he came out from behind a privacy screen toward the back of the room.

The air in here smelled immaculately clean and a scent of cinnamon spice wafted through the air. More white and blue Styrofoam snowflakes hung from the ceiling, giving the air of a winter storm. On a nearby wall shelf several fat red candles were lit, and Roxie guessed that's where the cinnamon smell came from.

The room looked like a real doctor's examination room, complete with metal shelves containing heavy-duty glass jars filled with cotton, lubrication bottles, latex gloves, ropes and much more. She swallowed when she spied an instrument tray on a rollaway cart in one corner. But before she could get a closer look, Evan's hot hand returned to her lower back and he ushered her to behind the privacy screen at the far end of the room.

"Before we begin, I want you to fully undress and use the paper sheet on the table to cover yourself. Leave the plug in and then lie on the exam table, feet in the stirrups, ass as close to the edge as possible. The doctors will be with you in just a few minutes."

Roxie nodded jerkily and watched him leave.

Sweet pete! She was going to self combust! Or faint from nerves.

On wobbly legs, she moved further behind the privacy screen. It was a room in itself back here. A metal shelf against the wall was piled high with neatly folded pale green and white colored linens. A padded gynecological exam table took up most of the space. It gleamed at her as she surveyed it. Silver metal and black padding, complete with stirrups, made it look pretty much the same as what she'd find when she went to the doctor.

It had a padded headrest and Roxie spied the heavy duty leather straps and restraints hanging off the sides of the table.

Oh boy, she thought to herself and blew out a tense breath. *What had she gotten herself into?*

To her surprise a full-length mirror, similar to the one in the upstairs changing room, hung on a nearby post. Fully facing it, she gazed at her reflection, gasping at the lusty green-eyed stranger staring back at her. Her hair appeared as a wild, sexy mess. She couldn't resist but to push her fingers through her strands to make herself more presentable. Her cheeks looked the rosiest she'd ever seen them and her mouth appeared swollen and red from Evan's kiss. She wished she *had* opened her mouth and let him in. Next time, she promised herself. Next time she would let him in and experience what pleasures he had to offer.

Her breasts boldly pressed against the tight latex and she swore her areolas looked bigger than lollipops as they burst against the fabric. She could still feel the imprint of Evan's hands on her breasts too. Such hot, big hands.

She kicked off her shoes, grateful to be out of the heels. She was used to wearing running shoes, not sexy ankle killers. Continuing to stare at the mirror—truth be told, she couldn't stop looking at her transformation—she reached up and pulled on the zipper. The raspy sound of it lowering split through the quiet air and she could imagine Brody and Evan on the other side of the screen, listening.

Roxie swallowed as another shot of nervousness shot through her. She forced herself to remain calm as she unzipped the suit the entire length right down to her mons. Peeling the smooth material aside, she allowed her breasts to spill free.

Gosh, they really did look big and swollen, obviously reacting to his touch. Her nipples were large and red. She touched her right nipple, finding it tender. Smoothing her hand under her breast, much the same way Evan did, she lifted it, testing the heaviness.

Blowing out a tense breath, she let go of her breast and proceeded to peel the suit over her shoulders and then lowered it over her hips and down her legs, stepping out of it as it puddled on the floor. Picking it up, she noticed the crotch area was damp from her arousal. Very damp.

Quickly she folded it and placed it neatly on an open shelf, placing her shoes beneath it and out of the way.

Once again she inspected herself in the mirror, her gaze moving to her lower half this time. Would both men be pleased with her nude pussy? She kept herself immaculately nude down there, knowing that without hair she could feel sensations more than when she wasn't bare. She dare not touch her pussy, for she could feel it swollen and pouty, the wetness pooling between her thighs.

Her hand fell upon the delicate paper sheet she would need to cover herself. As she got up on the table, the paper beneath her ass rustled and as she covered herself with the sheet, it crinkled too, giving away she was readying herself. The thing was practically see through and as she looked down she saw the outline of her nipples poking proudly against the soft paper. In this new position she could also feel the sharp push of the plug moving deeper into her anus, a gentle reminder of what would happen tonight.

She could hardly wait to experience two men impaling her. Despite her enthusiasm, Roxie tensed when she spied twin shadows against the privacy screen.

They were coming for her. Oh God.

Her heart pounded faster as the screen rolled away. Evan stood there, staring down at her, while Brody rolled the screen to the far side of the room. Fire and desire danced in Evan's eyes and splashed over her skin, spreading down her body to between her thighs.

"Looks like our patient is flushed, Doctor," Evan replied in a sultry voice that had all her nerve endings tensing and taking notice. "We need to take her temperature. I suspect a fever."

"Only one way to diffuse a fever, Dr. Evan," Brody replied.

The squeak of wheels followed. Because Evan stood so big and tall beside the bed, he blocked her view. She suspected he was bringing that rollaway cart she'd seen earlier.

"Open your mouth, sweetness," Evan instructed, then turned his back for a moment toward the cart behind him. When he turned around, he held what at first she believed to be a red and white candy cane but then realized it was actually a digital thermometer. She watched as he wiped it with a cotton ball. It smelled of peppermint.

When he aimed it at her mouth, she opened and lifted her tongue allowing the end of the thermometer to settle there.

His calloused thumb lingered along her bottom lip, stroking her softly. The urge to dart out her tongue and lick him hit hard. Before she could do it, he dropped his hand away. He turned and both men hunkered over that cart again.

"We'll start with a breast exam. Do you concur, Dr. Evan?" Brody's voice sounded thick and sultry.

"I concur, Dr. Brody. A breast exam sounds quite appropriate under the circumstances."

The digital thermometer in her mouth beeped and both men returned their attention to her.

Her heart thumped a mile a minute as Brody removed it.

"Most definitely a fever. Miss Roxie, you seem to be all hot and bothered. You'll need a complete physical examination before we can administer the cure."

"And what is the cure, doctors?" she breathed.

Both men looked at each other, then back at her.

She swallowed at their heated looks.

"The only way to douse a fever is to meet fever with fire. Lots of sultry fire administered by two doctors," Evan whispered.

Oh dear me. Oh dear my.

Another flush of heat burst through her as Brody came to the other side of the table where she lay.

"Dr. Evan, please do the honors," Brody instructed.

Roxie realized she was trembling again. Very nicely trembling and as Evan drew the paper sheet down, warm air brushed her breasts.

"Beautiful," Brody whispered. His voice throbbed with lust. She breathed in roughly as Evan stared down at her nakedness.

"I've been dying to see you splayed out like this from the moment I heard you were going to be a patient," Evan said. The deep and dark timbre lacing his voice had her feet pressing involuntarily against the stirrups.

He reached out and cupped the breast closest to him, his hand hot like a volcano, his fingers gripping her nipple with tender pressure and her eyes widened as he leaned forward and drew her nipple into his mouth.

He sucked her, taking deep hard draws. The intensity of the sharp pressure made her gasp as nerve endings snapped to life. He looked gorgeous sucking at her breast and she couldn't help but reach out and caress the roughness of his beard-shadowed cheek. His skin felt like fire beneath her fingertips and he groaned at her touch, the erotic sound playing like lightning over her nerve endings.

"Looks like you have a breast man on your hands, Ms. Roxie," Brody commented. She ripped her gaze from Evan and found Brody's brown eyes twinkling with amusement as he watched her. Warmth blushed through her like a brushfire.

"Your eyes indicate you need some cooling off. I'll just have to help Dr. Evan with his examination."

Brody cupped her other breast, his calloused hand feeling quite nice against her flesh and he tweaked her nipple with his thumb and forefinger bringing her to this side of pain before licking her taut flesh with his tongue. The featherlight touch had her arching her upper back for more. Thankfully, he enveloped her nipple, taking her between his warm lips. Her sensitive nipples throbbed in their mouths and she could feel the pleasure tension bursting in her breasts as it spread into her lower abdomen.

Two tongues caressed and she whimpered at the erotic sensations. Twin peaks of electricity lashed and bit, making her squirm against the sinful sensations, and once again she pushed her feet against the stirrups, wishing for one of them to drop a head between her thighs.

Trying to distract herself from that intoxicating thought, she reached out and caressed Brody's face as well, remembering Gina telling her that her ex-husband would be a tender yet dominant lover. The few times her roommate had spoken about Brody, Roxie had picked up the love in her voice for him. She didn't understand why Gina had divorced him and didn't understand why she wouldn't be jealous knowing her ex would be having sex with her roommate. If anything, Gina seemed turned on by that idea.

Roxie doubted if she could be so giving with Evan.

She moaned out loud at that thought. Oh God, she needed to stop thinking of Evan as hers. He didn't belong to her. They barely knew each other. Tonight was just sex and lust. Right? Right.

Chapter Four

Her body grew tighter and her nipples more sensitive. She'd never had two men sucking her breasts before. Intoxicating would be the word for it.

She watched in awed wonder as both men, one dirty blond, the other dark brown haired, their eyes closed, their full lips moving erotically as they licked and sucked and tenderly bit her nipples. She caught glimpses of how engorged and red her flesh had become beneath their succulent mouths. Could feel a whirlwind of erotic heat splashing around her, enveloping her, embracing her. Her thoughts disintegrated, her body took over, enjoying and bucking and wanting more.

"I've fantasized about you being my patient," Evan said around her nipple. His dark brown eyes were almost black now and heavy lidded from lust. His lips caressed her nipple and she yelped as he nibbled a bit too roughly, but she creamed despite the hurt.

As if Evan had made her cry out on purpose to give Brody a sign, both men let go of her and returned to the rollaway cart. Looking down at herself, she creamed again at the sight of her heaving swollen breasts. Her nipples were so red and so peaked. She didn't even recognize they belonged to her.

"Before we go any further with the exam, Dr. Evan, we need to restrain our patient," Brody said. Sexual hunger flared in Evan's eyes as he nodded.

Roxie blew out a tense breath. On the list of things to expect that Gina had given her, there would be a good possibility the men would wish to restrain her. The idea had turned Roxie on at the time, in reality though, she wasn't so sure as a sudden shot of nerves jumbled through her.

Trust them, Roxie. Trust them, an inner voice whispered.

She almost laughed at that thought. Her? Trust? She'd always had a problem with trust but now she would submit. Yes, she could trust them to bind her.

"Safe word," she whispered, letting them know she just might have an issue being bound by a couple of men she barely knew.

"What would you like it to be, sweetness?" Concern swept through Evan's face but she smiled reassuringly.

She was okay. She would be fine. It would be fun and erotic.

"Fire," she whispered.

"Fire it is," Brody growled and smiled down at her as he came around to the other side of her bed once again. He held a couple of plastic cones in his hands and she recognized them as breast pumps. She'd never experienced using them before so this should be interesting.

She watched as Evan tenderly tied her wrist with the heavy-duty leather restraint she'd seen dangling off the side of the bed earlier. On the other side of the bed, Brody did the same. When they finished, she tested them for strength. They barely moved an inch.

Shit.

"She's ready for her breast pumps, doctor." Evan winked down at her.

Oh God.

"These will keep you aroused while we do your pelvic examination," Evan reassured. He produced a tube of lube and squirted a liberal amount onto one palm. He took his time as he smoothed generous amounts of lube at the outer edges of her breasts, then Evan stood back.

"You may do the honors, doctor," Evan instructed.

Brody moved forward, his gaze intent and serious as he placed first one and then the other plastic cup over her breasts. The edges of the plastic fit perfectly over the lubed areas and he pressed down gently then moved the cups until suction occurred. She noticed clear plastic tubes protruding from the top of each cup. He handed the tubes to

Evan who rearranged them then brought them along the side of the bed to the cart where he plugged the ends into a machine.

"You're going to feel some pressure and then a sucking sensation," Evan said as he fiddled with a dial on the machine.

God, she felt as if she'd been dumped into some sort of science fiction movie, Roxie thought as she gazed at her pump-covered breasts. Damn if this sight wasn't turning her on even more!

Evan could barely restrain himself. Heat flared through his body and his breathing was ragged and raspy. The blood pounded through his veins, heading to parts south, engorging his cock and balls until the pressure was literally making him grit his teeth to keep from groaning. Roxie looked riveting splayed out on the gyno table with her legs spread, her bare feet in stirrups, and her arms helplessly at her sides bound with leather restraints.

Her skin was so damn soft, his fingers ached to caress every inch of her. And her breasts, man, he'd never seen such beautifully shaped breasts. Never touched such perfect red nipples. He could still feel their hardness in his mouth. Could still taste the sweet flesh as he'd licked and sucked and sipped the taut point.

He was, he realized, aware of every move she made. The way the paper sheet shifted over her lower half every time she so much as moved. Every lick of her lip. Every lowering of her eyelashes and every scent of hers from the delicate smell of soap she used on her skin to the soft peach scent of her shampoo.

Most of all he noticed how erotically she'd tensed when he began drawing on her nipple. Tensed even more when Brody joined him. He'd felt her body heat coming off her in waves. Had enjoyed it when she'd arched her back wanting more from them.

And when he'd lifted his head from her breast and looked down at her face, he'd never seen such raw arousal on a woman's face before. Her eyes were sparkling with so much lust, he'd had to force himself to look away from her or he would have given her another kiss. Kissing her was not a good idea at the moment. He'd almost lost his self-control in the hallway, but she'd been so cute in that red latex get up, wearing that Santa Claus hat and those mistletoe earrings that he'd wanted to sip from her lips again.

Oh man, *that* kiss. Talk about devastating to his senses. And she was playing coy with him too in not letting him into her mouth with his tongue. Her hesitation, her shyness, intrigued him. Made him curious about her. Made him want her even more.

As the breast pumps sucked, her eyes glazed over with excitement and his cock jerked and throbbed as he imagined lowering the sheet that covered her lower half. His body felt tense, taut and when he glanced over at Brody, he could tell, his friend was having a similar reaction.

Brody's brown eyes flared with heat and his expression looked desperate. He was breathing just as harshly as Roxie and himself and Evan liked the way Brody looked at her. With caring and with a need to pleasure her and be pleasured inside of her.

He swallowed and lowered his gaze to the bulge between Brody's pants and he almost let out a whistle at the size of his erection. Roxie was definitely going to get a treat tonight from the both of them. Two nice big treats. He turned his attention to the sheet covering the rest of her. If the throbbing and the pleasure-pain lacing his balls and cock were an indication, they would need to hurry things along. And fast.

"It's getting way too hot in here, Dr. Brody," Evan said as he and Brody hovered over that cart again. When Roxie saw Evan nod to Brody and they started to remove their tops, she fought to breath. Oh gosh, he wasn't kidding. They were getting just as hot as she was. Her pulse quickened as Evan shed his top and Brody quickly followed. Trouble was they stopped after removing their tops. Not that there was anything wrong with that. Both men possessed exquisite muscular backs and just watching their bulging muscles in their vein-roped arms as they touched things on that tray had her panting softly as she anxiously awaited their next move.

"Before we continue, I need to check your heart rate, Miss Roxie," Evan said as he turned around and grinned at her. Her breath backed up in her lungs as she focused her attention to his wide chest. A light dusting of soft curly brown hair covered him there and those muscles in his arms were popping as he removed his mask and lifted the stethoscope from his neck. She licked her lips, wetting them as her mouth suddenly felt dry.

He leaned closer and his unique scent swept around her again. He smelled of sex and mystery and arousal all wrapped up in one wonderful package. She noticed the tiny red Christmas bow near the end of the stethoscope hugging the chest piece when he placed it just above her plastic covered right breast. How had she missed that little bow? she pondered as Evan stuffed the earpieces in his ears and listened.

She swallowed, licked her dry lips again. God, she hadn't realized it would be so arousing having a stethoscope on her naked body. Maybe she shouldn't have a female doctor to do her regular yearly physicals? That thought made her bite her lip. There was no way she was going to have a male doctor after what these two men were doing with her tonight. No way.

"She's pounding like the drummer boy beating on a drum, Doctor. I think it's time we begin her pelvic exam and give her another type of pounding."

She creamed at the visualization his words created. Naked flesh slapping against naked flesh. The suctioning sound of one man's cock entering her and another leaving.

Oh-my-God.

Evan winked at her and she saw a pink flush of excitement in his cheeks. He removed the stethoscope, hung it back around his neck again, giving her the impression he really was a doctor. Gosh, he looked so cute wearing a stethoscope. Kind of like McDreamy or maybe he looked more like McSteamy. His direct gaze never left her face as he stalked along the side of the gyno table and joined Brody at the foot.

If her heart had been pounding loudly before, then Evan should hear it even more now, she thought as she tensed and her feet pressed even harder against the metal stirrups while she awaited their next move.

"Do the honors, Dr. Brody." Evan's voice was filled with tension and both men's Adam's apples bobbed as Brody reached out and torturously slowly pulled the paper sheet off her. She held her breath as the paper sensually rubbed along her belly, then along her thighs, to her hoisted knees and then down her legs, tickling her toes. Then the sheet was gone and both men were gazing between her spread thighs.

"Fuck," Brody whispered.

"Fucking fantastic," Evan breathed.

They stared at her, their eyes growing darker by the second. Warmth scuttled around her pussy and she creamed. She couldn't stop herself from trembling again as desire whipped through her. She didn't know why she was shaking up a storm tonight. She'd never done that before. Heck, no one had affected her as much as Evan. Too bad she'd never told him that. She would make a point of it.

After tonight.

Maybe.

No, she was a swinger. No strings sex. She needed to remember that. Oh boy, did she ever need to remember that.

"Very pretty," Brody whispered.

"My pretty," Evan whispered back. The tip of his tongue peeked out of his mouth and he wet his bottom lip.

"You take her blood pressure, doctor. I'll begin the exam," Evan directed.

As Evan stepped closer to the foot of the bed, she noticed he held something in his hand. Something metal with a handle and on the other end a...pinwheel?

"The pinwheel will increase your sensations," Brody acknowledged as he placed the blood pressure cuff around her upper right arm and pumped.

She yelped in surprise as a delicate trail of pinpricks ran up the inside of her right inner thigh toward her pussy.

Oh this feels wonderful. Further up. Come on. Bring it over my clit.

She moaned her disappointment when he headed the pinwheel away from her pussy, over her mons and down the inside of her other thigh. Then he came up again, the pinwheel causing the sweetest sense of anticipation as it neared her pussy again. Then he swept it over her mons and down the other side.

She cursed softly.

Evan smiled, mischievousness melting the arousal that glowed in his almost black eyes.

"Blood pressure is going up, Doctor. Keep up the great work," Brody said and a moment later released the cuff from her arm and headed back to the cart.

He rummaged through the top tray, grabbed something, which she couldn't get a good look at, and handed it to Evan, who in turn gave Brody the pinwheel. Then Brody came to the top of the bed and began running the pinwheel along the sides of her neck and over her chest in a delicate manner. If he meant to distract her from what was going on between her legs, it wasn't working.

She watched as Evan looked down and when his fingers parted her labia, she whimpered at his delicate touch.

"In a minute we'll be able to get a nice up close look at your pussy," Evan said.

Close up look at her pussy! Oh my gosh!

Reaching out, he pulled a floor lamp close, flicked it on and aimed the light between her thighs. She could feel the heat of the bulb, even with it being four feet away. Could feel the heat of his fingers as he massaged her labia with his fingers coming so close to her clit that she couldn't help but want to close her legs and trap him against her pussy and squeeze herself into an orgasm.

"No, no, darling. Don't move your legs," Brody commanded in a voice so thick with emotion it sent erotic spirals up her spine.

She bit her top lip and pressed her feet against the stirrups in an effort to keep her legs spread.

With her pussy lips being massaged by Evan, she felt plump and swollen. A moment later there were a few tugs and some pressure on her labia. Then more pulling, until they stretched and slightly burned.

"What...what are you doing?" she couldn't help but ask.

"Clamping you open for whatever pleasures I wish to give, sweetness." Evan's expression looked desperate, yet his voice sounded oddly calm, controlled. Gosh, she was getting wild with need and these two doctors seemed to be toying with her with all these contraptions.

I want sex. Not toys, a frustrated voice shouted in her mind.

To Roxie's surprise, Brody dipped a finger into her mouth and she accepted it with ease, wanting it, needing it. He slipped the finger between her teeth and played with her tongue.

Gosh, this felt so erotic.

"You're wide open for oral, now."

Sweet mercy, did he have to be so descriptive? Her mind whirled as she envisioned how her pussy lips would look, plump and stretched with clamps, allowing Evan to see the opening to her vagina. That vision made her instinctively press her lips tighter around Brody's finger as he seductively plunged it in and out of her mouth like a miniature cock. He moaned as her teeth rasped him every time he came in, the sound of his voice animalist and raw.

Her eyelids were growing heavy too as the pleasure burn stretched through her labia and through a sexual haze she watched Evan getting down on his knees, his head disappearing between her thighs.

Chapter Five

Roxie moaned as Evan's hot breath blasted against her pussy. Cried out as a tongue kissed her throbbing clitoris in a featherlight touch. Involuntarily she arched her hips, exquisite sensations rippling through her body. The intoxicating kiss was followed by his tongue lapping at her clit. More sensations exploded and she moaned around Brody's finger.

"Oh man, she's killing me here, Dr. Evan. I'm going to need some relief soon." Brody's guttural voice called from somewhere above her. She struggled to keep her eyes open but couldn't. She closed them and allowed herself to feel what was happening between her legs while she sucked on Brody's finger.

Up until now the breast pumps had been only a minor distraction but she now noticed Brody had removed the pinwheel. Suction suddenly increased beneath the breast pumps. He must have turned up the pressure, she thought and wow, it felt incredible. Okay, so maybe she could accept these toys because they sure were heightening her senses.

Evan's tongue slid into her vagina. She trembled and shook and creamed from the intimate invasion. He plunged into her vagina again, dipped out, his wet tongue smoothing faster and harder over her clit, lashing her with excruciating sensations.

"Evan," she gasped frantically, feeling the orgasm drawing closer.

"Hold on, sweetness, give him a little more time. Here's another finger for you to suck on." Brody dipped a second finger into her mouth, and she easily accepted it, sucking on the two digits, feeling her pussy contract as Evan suddenly slipped two fingers into her vagina.

"Oh!" she cried out as Evan's fingers thrust, his tongue dabbing and massaging her clit with such force he drove her closer to the edge. Just as she was about to give in to the wonderful explosion she knew was ready to rock her world, they both stopped.

"Fuck!" she cried out her disappointment loud and hard. Her feet pressed into the stirrups with protest and she pulled on the restraints, feeling the need to be fucked roaring up inside her like a lion.

"Hang on baby, hang on," Evan called out through the frustrating fog that clutched her now. She could hear the sounds of zippers lowering. Jeans moving past hips. And then she heard something being pulled along the floor to her right side and forced open her eyes to see Brody pulling over a stool and Evan standing between her thighs, his hugely engorged cock held in his hand. The look on his face was tortured, yet he was smiling down at her.

"You do oral on Brody. Relieve him," he commanded.

She nodded in submission, whimpering, knowing a good fucking was going to be delayed. She turned her head toward Brody who had climbed on the stool, his engorged cock, just as huge as Evan's, was merely an inch from her mouth. Willingly she opened her mouth and accepted his cock. He slid between her lips, his girth large enough to make them stretch. His cock head was flushed with heat and as round and silky as a plum, his shaft hard and powerful as he slid in. She stroked him with her tongue, exploring the elevated veins, drawing him in further, enjoying the sound of his harsh intake of breath as she took him as far in as she could.

He reached down and clasped a hand around his shaft preventing himself from going too deep, then he withdrew and thrust into her mouth again. She lashed the ultra sensitive soft area beneath his cock head with her tongue and loved the way his face contorted with pleasure.

"Fuck, she looks really nice with a cock in her mouth, Dr. Evan. Really nice."

"Just remember she belongs to me," Evan growled back. She liked the way his voice sounded territorial and dark.

Brody chuckled back, obviously enjoying this side of Evan too.

He pumped between her lips and she accepted him thrust for thrust, sucking him hard and letting him go with a pop every time he withdrew. She watched his balls bounce as his thighs trembled and sucked him harder, wanting to give him the pleasure.

She moaned around Brody's cock as Evan thrust a couple of fingers into her. He withdrew and drove into her again, making sure his knuckle rubbed nicely against her clit. A third time in and she gagged as she exploded, the climax destroying her senses, the snap of electricity burning over her damp flesh. Erotic spasms rippled through her pussy making her shake from the deep sensuality of it.

From somewhere far away she heard Brody moan and warn her he was coming. His cock swelled against her lips and his heavy flesh jerked in her mouth, his release spurting warm jets down her throat.

Evan swore he was going to lose it. Watching Brody fucking Roxie's mouth while she came undone was the most erotic sight he'd ever seen. She looked so damn pretty with cock in her mouth. With every buck of her hips, his hold on his self-control diminished. With every spasm of her cunt muscles that clenched his fingers, his balls and cock tightened. With her every moan around Brody's erection, his desperation raged.

He wanted Roxie and he wanted her now!

But she was climaxing and he wanted to make it the best he could for her. She was coming apart, her body writhing and wrenching with each sensual spasm. Her moans urged him to pump harder. He thrust into her with fast, even strokes and watched perspiration blossom over her flushed pink skin. The girl was on fire. Blazing hot. Melting into a boiling pot of pleasure.

Man. He needed her bad.

Emotions spiraled through him. Thick and urgent. He plunged faster, stroked into her until he could feel the spasms ebb. Until Brody was finished.

Now it would be his turn to take her.

They removed the breast pumps, the clamps and her restraints, laid her on her belly and then the fun began. The spanking. The blushing ass. Brody watched as Evan spanked her. With every slap of his hand against her blushing ass, her body shook and her ass cheeks flushed a brighter pink. Her cries sounded sultry and soft and he knew she enjoyed it. With her every cry he grew harder until he swore he could no longer contain himself. But he did. Forced himself to.

Tonight he was a third. Evan wanted Roxie and tonight was a gift to her. When Roxie and Evan grew closer in their relationship, and Brody knew they would as the signs were all there. Them sneaking glances at each other when they thought the other wasn't watching and then coming together now in this untraditional way, Brody knew in his heart they would get their happily ever after. They had probably been in bad relationships and weren't able to trust their attraction for each other. Maybe they just weren't sure of each other. Hell, they were off to a pretty good start with Evan forking out all that cash for her, when he probably needed it to fix up that old farmhouse he'd purchased.

Tonight was all about pleasure. Hers and Evan's and his.

She jerked again as Evan smacked her ass one more time. Then Brody lowered his head and kissed each blushing ass cheek as gently as a feather. He could see Roxie's body melting against his tender light touches. Could see she trusted him now. When Evan's fingers touched upon the white base of her butt plug, Brody groaned at the fever raging inside him. A fever that could only be extinguished in one way.

Roxie felt Evan part her ass cheeks and she lost what little self-control she'd been hanging onto.

"Evan!" she called out in a voice that sounded tormented now. But she liked this wild woman in herself. Absolute freedom. And trust.

"Just a minute, Roxie. Just...one more... minute, baby," Evan reassured.

The plug moved slowly as he gripped the base. Gently, he pulled, and her ass clenched tightly around the plug, protesting, trying to keep it buried inside her.

He pulled harder and she inhaled as the pressure mounted and moved out of her with a soft suctioning pop. Then two sets of hands were helping her onto her wobbly legs. Her ass burned nicely from the slaps and wetness drenched her pussy. She hadn't realized a spanking by Evan would feel so sensual. She'd had other guys spank her but truly hadn't felt this turned on. As Evan stood in front of her, she met his gaze. She saw the lust, the excitement. It was the same need she felt inside. All those emotions were blazing and she could feel them zipping through her too.

When she looked in that mirror hanging on the nearby wall, she couldn't help but whimper as Brody dropped to his knees behind her. His eyes raged with raw lust and wicked intent as his hot palms smoothed tenderly over the curves of her ass. She loved his touch and melted into his caresses, moaning when sharp teeth raked her tender flesh.

"Enjoying yourself, aren't you?" Evan asked, his voice sounding so primal, the desire in his eyes flaring so deeply, it was truly a savage expression.

She nodded, feeling the tension zipping between all three of them. Reaching out, she took Evan's cock into her hands. He was big and heavy. The elevated web of veins throbbed against her fingertips and she squeezed his swollen erection enjoying the way he scrunched his eyes shut and groaned. She moved her hands beneath his cock and held his sac, squeezing and twisting gently.

"Roxie," he said in a warning tone, insinuating she'd better be careful.

"Your turn to trust me," she whispered and squeezed and kneaded his sac until he reached up and curled his fingers over her shoulders.

"Feels good, doesn't it?" she breathed and leaned forward as Brody kissed her heated ass. She continued kissing Evan and she kind of liked that he wasn't kissing back, probably because she literally had him by the balls.

"How's this kiss?" she said, teasing the side of his mouth where she spied a small scar.

He didn't say anything, but she could tell he liked it in the way he breathed raggedly.

"How'd you get it?" she asked.

"What?"

She could feel the tension in his chest as she rubbed her breasts against his muscles.

"The scar." She kissed along the edge of his jaw down to beneath his chin and felt the mad pound of his pulse against her lips.

"Happened when I was a kid," he said in gasps. He stopped talking when her hands left his sac and wrapped again around his cock. From previous experience she knew some guys liked their cocks twisted, and she wondered if Evan was one of them.

She twisted and squeezed. Hard.

He swore softly, his fingers digging like daggers into her shoulders.

Yes, he definitely enjoyed a little pain with his pleasure.

"So what happened?" She kissed her way along his corded neck and across his damp collarbone, loving the way he smelled of sweat and soap. He tensed as she twisted and untwisted his cock as if she were wringing her pantyhose.

She'd definitely like to get this guy into her shower with her and hold his wrists hostage with pantyhose while she went down on him under a steamy, hot spray.

Focus, Roxie. Focus.

When she took his hard, pebbled nipple into her mouth, he gasped.

"Was shoveling snow with a friend," he whispered quickly.

His fingers loosened on her shoulders.

"He lifted his shovel a bit too high and I was too close and bam, three stitches."

He sucked in a breath as she bit his nipple. The hard tender flesh held captive between her teeth while she lashed it with her tongue.

Evan's hands left her shoulders, slid up her neck and splayed into her hair. She winced as pain shot through her scalp as his fingers tangled with her strands. He held her head steady and forced her away from his nipple.

Hmm, very delicate erotic zone, she'd have to remember that for another time. And there was definitely going to be more times if she got her way.

"Tonight is all about pleasuring you, sweetness. All about you," he breathed. The tips of his mouth tilted upward in such a heartwarming smile, Roxie's breath caught in her throat. He looked so sexy when he smiled. He should do it more often.

"Hold her steady, now," Brody warned from behind her. Roxie tensed as Evan cupped the back of her head and gazed into her eyes. She heard the sound of foil being ripped open and the soft whoosh of a condom being rolled on. Slurpy sounds of lube.

"We're going to give you what you came for. Just remember that you belong to me afterward."

She nodded numbly, thrilled that he wished to continue seeing her when tonight was over.

He let go of her and she watched as he reached for a sealed condom on the nearby cart. He ripped it open then rolled it on. His hands came back to her face again, his fingers caressing her cheeks, his intense gaze watching her face.

She gasped at the unbelievable pressure and squeezed her eyes shut as Brody's lubed cock head pushed against her sphincter. She felt Evan's thick cock pressing against her vaginal opening at the same time and tensed. How could she take both men at the same time? Was that even possible?

Her eyes popped open as a slice of panic shot through her.

"Shh, relax, sweetness," Evan whispered, his hot breath feathering across her face and his mouth danced over hers in an electrifying kiss. Instinctively she parted her lips, wanting him to enter and gasped as his hands dropped from her face, over her shoulders, trailing down her arms to land upon her hips.

His kiss deepened and he plunged into her mouth, the impact of their tongues snapping together rocking her to her core. She moaned into his mouth, the erotic sound gurgled and strangled.

Brody's cock slid in further. The tight clench of Roxie's muscles gave way, slowly accommodating Brody's penis.

Thankfully, Evan's cock head stayed poised at her vaginal opening, partially buried inside her.

Evan broke the intoxicating kiss and licked and nipped gently at her lips. "You taste sweet and hot. I knew you would. Fantasized you would. Just like I know you're going to feel real nice wrapped around my cock. And Evan's cock. Your hot body sandwiched between us while we fuck you over and over."

His words feathered against her mouth, creating wicked visions. Struggling to open her eyes, she managed to turn her head and watch in the mirror. Watched as her heavy lids struggled to stay open while a naked man pressed against her entire backside, his face buried in the back of her neck. While another naked man's body melted against hers, his hands like brands on her hips, his gaze meeting hers in the mirror.

"You look hot, sweetness. Hot between two men. Just as I knew you would."

She moaned as Brody's head turned and met their gazes. His eyes flared with lust, his large hands were on her shoulders, his hips thrusting forward in a solid push that had his cock coming into her.

She gritted her teeth, took the full bite of the pleasure-pain, the wanton pressure.

She was panting now. Her skin flushed with heat and need. Her eyelids so heavy she had to struggle to keep them open just to watch the erotic sight of the two men wrapped around her body.

Oh wow, she'd truly never seen anything or experienced something so erotic in her life.

Excitement burst through her as Evan's cock, hard as steel, swollen with heat, pushed into her vagina.

"Tight," he moaned. "So tight."

Brody withdrew, and then Evan quickly followed. Shudders spun through her as both men came in again. Then they started pumping.

The fierceness of their combined thrusts caused such a magnificent friction, Roxie could feel the heat zip through the air around them. Pleasure seared through her and she struggled to keep it from coming full on. Their grunts and the slaps of flesh upon her flesh, as they both thrust their hips against hers, sent intoxicating messages into her brain.

Yeah, she could get used to this kind of fucking. Really used to it.

Their thrusts into her became harder, fiercer, more determined. The raw shocks of their flesh sliding over hers snapped her nerve endings like live wires, hurling her closer to the edge. Tension built inside her womb, raged through her body with fever speed.

They drove into her like two unwavering pistons. Hot, sultry, powerful. There was no use in trying to keep the orgasm from coming any longer. No use in staying in the heady excitement of pre-climax.

She let go.

Sensations snapped through her every fiber, tightening her body to the point where she had never been so tense. Their driving plunges continued. Their hoarse cries mingled with hers, their flesh slapping against her, into her, and the onslaught of emotions and spasms pushed her past her breaking point into the fragmented world of pleasure and pain.

Shudders claimed her senses. Smashed any shred of self-control and Roxie knew she'd probably never be the same again. She rode the crest of searing waves. Rode them hard. And when it was finally over, weariness claimed them. They held her and rocked with her, murmuring wonderful words of encouragement and satisfaction.

She'd trusted them. And for the first time in her life, Roxie truly knew the meaning of the words feeling free.

* * * * *

The song *I'll be Home for Christmas* sifted through the toasty interior of Evan's battered old GM pickup truck. The buttery glow of headlights barely cut through the blinding whirlwind of snowflakes that snapped like little heartbeats against his windshield. Despite his white knuckled grip on the steering wheel and the crunch of newly accumulated foot high snow on the desolate road that would lead him to his farmhouse, he couldn't stop smiling.

Beside him, Roxie slept. He'd been pleasantly surprised tonight when after Brody left the medical examination room, Evan asked her if she wanted to pick up where they left off back at his farmhouse, and she'd said yes. When they'd bundled up and headed outside to find the snowstorm blowing white all around the parking lot, she'd giggled, stuck out her tongue and caught the snowflakes. He swore he'd fallen in love with her right then and there. Hell, he was lying. He'd already fallen in love with her the minute he'd seen her his first day of work when he'd watched her working on the line, wiping fingerprints off the RV hoods with alcohol before the vehicles entered the paint booth. He'd seen she was a hard worker. He liked that in a woman. It showed character and determination.

They would be good together. He just knew it.

When he pulled up before his two story farmhouse, he was glad he'd left his Christmas lights on. The twinkling glow of yellow, green, blue and red made the old farmhouse look welcome and bright.

"It's beautiful," he heard her whisper. There was awe in her voice and that impressed him too. When he'd bought the place, he'd known it would require a lot of work. Had expected he wouldn't bring her here until he'd fixed it up. But after tonight, he just wanted her with him.

Always.

Roxie stretched and inhaled as naughty little aches zipped through her pussy and backside. Despite the soreness, it felt good. Who knew getting fucked by two men would make her feel so liberated?

Awesome.

And the white clapboard farmhouse in front of her looked breathtaking. A lonely two-story building with a white picket fence. Okay, so maybe because of all the snow plastering the roof and everywhere, the house might be another color but hey, if she got her way, that farmhouse would be white and so would the fence.

And in the background, through the swirling snowflakes she spied a dark ominous building. The barn, she presumed. It would be painted red. Yeah, a red barn.

"What are you smiling at?" Evan asked as he switched off the Christmas music and turned off the truck.

"You," she whispered. "I'm smiling at you because I feel like I've just come home."

Gosh, where had those words come from?

She expected him to jolt and start up the car and bring her back to the club's parking lot and for him to tell her she was moving way too fast.

Maybe she was, but it just felt right to tell him what she felt. Felt right to trust him.

He grinned, that awesome smile that made her heart leap with joy.

"You know what? I've been thinking the same thing. Call me crazy or maybe that's why I was so damn scared shitless to ask you out on a real date, because something was telling me that you are the girl for me."

Surprise breezed through Roxie at his comment.

Evan shook his head and frowned, staring at her, almost willing her to understand.

"Am I making sense?" he asked.

Hell no.

She could read what she figured to be desperation in his eyes. As if he were hoping she wouldn't think he was totally nuts or was some insane serial killer or something.

"I mean we barely know each other and this might sound crazy but it runs in my family."

Roxie blinked in puzzlement. "Okay, you lost me. What runs in your family?"

Being crazy? Oh no, that would just be her luck for him to be crazy.

"It happened to my brother, to my dad and to my sister. This love at first sight thing. It's the family curse."

Shit.

The truck shuddered as a blast of wind snapped against it. But Roxie didn't quite feel it from the shock of hearing his confession.

Love at first sight was the family curse?

Oh man, had she been dropped into some freaking fantasy world or something?

"You look stunned. I guess I shouldn't have dropped it on you like this."

Roxie couldn't help but laugh. "I think family curses like that are just what I need. There's nothing more in the world that I would love than to wake up every Christmas morning with you, Evan."

He looked properly shocked.

"And tomorrow morning will just happen to be the first Christmas," she said boldly, loving this newfound freedom he'd given to her.

"A hot, sexy woman for Christmas. I like the sound of that," Evan said. His eyes twinkled and he leaned over, his hands tangling in her hair.

When his mouth melted over hers like white-hot lava, Roxie once again felt as if she'd finally come home.

Want more Jan Springer Adult Romances?

Mini Catalog

Boxed Sets

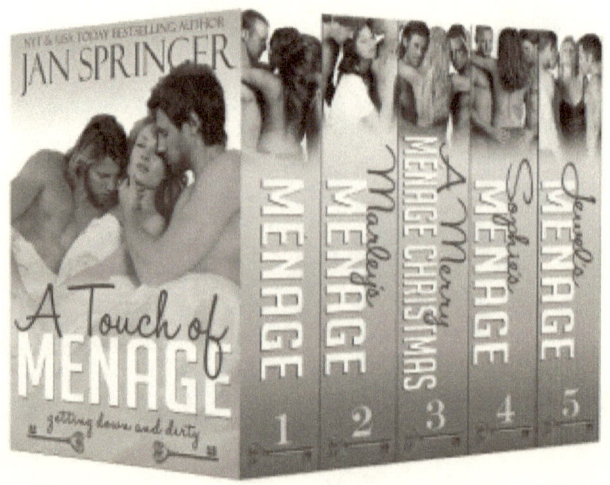

SIX Erotic Romance Ménage Stories! INCLUDES A BONUS MÉNAGE EBOOK

BONUS MENAGE BOOK: "Cowboys for Christmas," Book one of Jan's new Cowboys Online series. Jennifer Jane is getting THREE Cowboys for Christmas. What more could a girl want?
Jennifer Jane Watson has spent the past ten Christmases in a maximum-security prison. The last thing she expects is to get early parole along with a job on a secluded Canadian cattle ranch serving Christmas holiday dinners to three of the sexiest cowboys she's ever met!

~

Step into The Key Club's Ménage Nights where naughty fantasies come true and two men are hotter than one. Includes FIVE bestselling The Key Club stories; Ménage, Marley's Ménage, A Merry Ménage Christmas, Sophie's Ménage and Jewel's Ménage.

Includes The Key Club Series
Ménage - Book One

Sandwiched between constant deadlines, erotic romance author Claire Miller, enjoys an occasional unwind at The Key Club. And this time she's going to indulge in a yummy ménage.

Marley's Ménage - Book Two

Single soon-to-be mom Marley Madison has had some wicked cravings in her day, but being pregnant has made her cravings downright naughty. She wants a sizzling ménage and she needs it bad.

A Merry Ménage Christmas - Book Three

Dr. Kelsie Madison can't remember the last time she's had no-strings sex, and that's her clue she's been working way too hard. It's time to unwind at the Key Club by indulging in a yummy Christmas present for herself...a red-hot ménage.

Sophie's Ménage - Book Four

It's Spank-Me Ménage Night at the Key Club and Sophie is finally taking the plunge back into the spank scene...but she didn't expect her two ex-boyfriends to be there too.

Jewel's Ménage - Book Five

She thought she would never trust a man again...
Until one rainy night, two hunky truckers come to Jewel's rescue,
igniting delicious desires for a red-hot ménage a trios.

Other Books In the Key Club Series
(not included in this boxed set)
Jaxie's Ménage - Book Six

A close encounter with death pushes Jaxie into making one of her most intimate fantasies come true...

A Homecoming Ménage Christmas - Book Seven

Rachel has a very naughty secret, and she's way too embarrassed to let anyone know about it. When The Key Club throws a Santa Fetish Ménage Night, it's almost too good to be true. She has to figure out how to participate without anyone finding out!

Risqué Girl Delights Boxed Set
by Jan Springer

A touch of romance, a sizzling ménage, or...how about both?

What you'll find inside this Boxed Set:

Edible Delights
Toygasm
Shy Girl
Roman and Julietta

Edible Delights

(m/f/m Contemporary Erotic Romance Ménage)

Years ago, Allie Masters lost herself in the scorching passion of a ménage a trois relationship with her two bosses. In order to regain her independence, she walked away.

Max and Nick were very fulfilled with their gorgeous assistant. The lovemaking was breathtaking and both men willingly shared the woman they wanted to spend the rest of their lives with. Then she left.

Now Max and Nick have decided it's time to seduce Allie back into their lives.

Toygasm

(m/f/m Contemporary Erotic Romance Ménage)

It's a case of mistaken identity when the two owners of Sexy Toys show up for an erotic photo shoot of their toys with famous nude model Cammie Creek.

Cammie believes the two hunks are the male models she's supposed to work with. Usually she doesn't mix business with pleasure, but when they're seducing her right there in front of the camera, she can't resist turning them into her own personal naughty toys.

Josh and Jode are enjoying the perks of being male models—hot lust, sizzling toys and the best pleasure they've ever had. But how will Cammie react when she discovers they're actually her bosses and not just male models?

Shy Girl

(m/f Contemporary Erotic Romance with ménage scenes)
Finally free of an abusive relationship, shy girl Emma McCall sheds her inhibitions and explores her sensual side at Club Rendezvous, a swinger's club.

At the club she's surprised to find Logan Masters, a sexy hunk she's secretly fantasized about since college.

With Logan's help, Emma will experience her ultimate fantasy—a scorching ménage a trois.

Roman and Julietta

(m/f Contemporary Erotic Romance)

Her perfect lover...

Modern-day pirate Julietta Black's life has always been immersed in the violent and traditional ways of piracy. When her family's archenemy puts a hit out on her family, Julietta knows there's one sure way to lift the hit; she must kidnap the enemy's sexy grandson and literally force a union between the two warring families. Night after night, wrapped in Roman's strong arms, Julietta can't deny the searing attraction blazing between them. Nor can she deny he now holds her heart—as well as her life—in his hands.

His dream angel...

When Roman Prince's mysterious captor offers him a luscious woman to bed, fierce desire ignites, melting his usually tight self-control. Lust quickly turns to love as he enjoys their naughty trysts more than he should. How will he react when he discovers he's been kidnapped, not for a ransom, but captured for his sperm?

Pleasure Bound Box Set

The Complete Series

Books 1 - 6

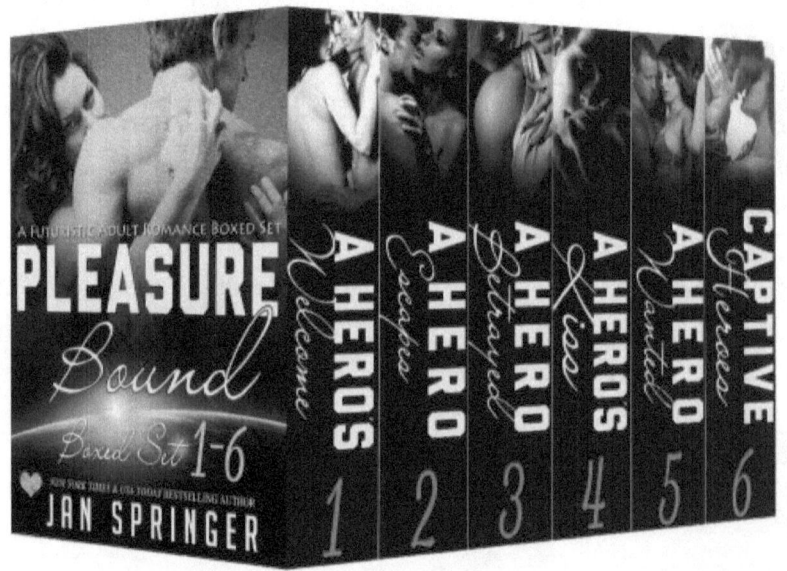

A Futuristic Adult Romance

Books 1-6

This PLEASURE BOUND BOXED SET is an EROTIC ROMANCE SET and includes the first SIX books in the Pleasure Bound series.

TOP-SECRET MISSION: Explore a recently discovered planet in outer space.

DISCOVERY: A sizzling trip into the realms of bondage, BDSM, pleasure-pain, betrayal and...love.
Inside this Boxed Set:
During a top-secret mission to a newly discovered planet, the six Hero siblings are thrust into a sensual world of erotic violence, unconventional romance and sizzling sex.

A HERO'S WELCOME

Pleasure Bound, Book One

Jan Springer

Being shot and held captive isn't what astronaut Joe Hero had in mind when he agreed to a top-secret mission to explore a newly discovered planet for NASA.

But a man would have to be dead not to fall for the sensual female doctor in charge of his care.

One night of scorching passion in the arms of the stranger from another planet is enough to convince Dr. Annie there's more to males than she's been taught by the Educators.

Who is this sexy hunk and why does she welcome him into her bed and her heart *every* chance she gets?

A HERO ESCAPES

Pleasure Bound, Book Two
Jan Springer
Queen Jacey has always fantasized about bedding a male.
But taking one for her enjoyment is strictly forbidden. That is, until an attractive well-hung stranger from another planet forces her to overcome her training and her beliefs.
Being held captive and forced to mate with a gorgeous Queen isn't exactly what astronaut Ben Hero expected when he agreed to explore a newly discovered planet for NASA.
Escaping *should* be his top priority but making sizzling love to Jacey *is* all he can think about.
When he discovers she's also being held captive, Ben's protective instincts kick in big time.
Suddenly they're on the run, irresistibly aroused, and wrapped in each other's arms every chance they get!

A HERO BETRAYED

Pleasure Bound, Book Three
Jan Springer
Astronaut Buck Hero didn't count on being held captive or becoming infected with passion poison when he agreed to explore a newly discovered planet for NASA.
If he doesn't get the cure soon he's going to be one *very* dead man.
Fugitive on-the-run Virgin has just rescued an infected male and needs to administer the cure - a twenty-four-hour sex marathon. Then she'll turn him over to his enemies in order to gain her freedom.
But her well-laid plans go into orbit when she discovers she's fallen in love with the stranger from another world.

A HERO'S KISS

Pleasure Bound, Book Four
Jan Springer
*During a secret NASA mission to locate their brothers on the faraway
planet of Paradise, the Hero sisters become separated after they
crash-land...and find unexpected romance with the tormented male
warriors of the species.*

Jarod and Piper

Being injured and infected by sensuous swamp water isn't what Piper Hero signed up for when she agreed to search for her three missing brothers. But when she's rescued by a dangerously sexy man who makes her so hot that she can't even think straight, Piper is glad that she came.

Jarod Ellis has sworn off women. But he's captivated by Piper Hero, a woman who claims to be related to the Earthmen he has vowed to protect with his life. Although he mistrusts her, she sets free a carnal inferno of needs he's never experienced during his previous life as a pleasure slave.

Despite her intimate fantasies coming true, Piper knows she needs to continue her mission of reuniting her siblings and she'll do it-with or without the help of her well-hung stud...

A HERO WANTED

Pleasure Bound, Book Five
(Loosely connected with this series)
Jan Springer

*Old-fashioned gal needs a man who loves to walk in the rain. Must be
well-hung. A homebody, white picket fence-type of guy. Sexual
requirements-gentle yet untamed lover. He must be sexually adventurous
who will train me to be same. Must be romantic, enjoy toys, interested in
mutual light bondage, ménages are welcome.*

That's what full-figured, antique shop owner Jenna MacLean wants
when she and her best friend outline a want ad just for fun on their
weekly girls' night out.

After years of being away from his pretty-plus sized ex-girlfriend,
Sully's back in town. When he finds the want ad, he knows he's the
only man who can make all of Jenna's sizzling-hot fantasies come true.
She's never left his heart and he needs her back in his bed—but he's
not going the traditional romantic route. This time, he'll prove he
loves her with help from the notorious Ménage Club, a relationship
club designed specifically to get estranged couples back together with
the help of a third and sometimes a fourth in the bedroom.

CAPTIVE HEROES

Pleasure Bound, Book Six
Jan Springer

During a secret NASA mission to locate their brothers on the faraway planet of Paradise, the Hero sisters become separated after they crash land...and find unexpected romance with the tormented alien male warriors of the species in this ultra-long sci-fi book.

Taylor and Kayla

While searching for her brothers, Kayla Hero is bound and imprisoned by the Breeders— along with a male captive whose tantalizing scars pique her interest. Forced to escape with him, she's irresistibly aroused when she suddenly becomes *his* captive. Wild lust flares in Kayla's eyes— a sensual side effect of the Fever Swamp water she's accidentally ingested. Taylor knows he will enjoy administering the cure — lots of sizzling hot lovemaking!

Blackie and Kinley

Injured and lost in a dense jungle, Kinley Hero is intimidated by the scarred man who hunts her, especially due to the power of erotic submission he holds over her.

Capturing his beautiful female prey, Blackie can't wait to train her as a pleasure slave for the Death Valley Boys. When her captor slips a collar around her neck, Kinley must struggle with lust as a natural submissive.

A CONTEMPORARY EROTIC ROMANCE BOXED SET

Naughty Girl Desires Boxed Set: Romance, Contemporary Romance, Romance Suspense, Box Set

(m/f only)

What You'll Find Inside Naughty Girl Desires

Jade's Fantasy

Kidnap Fantasies, Book One

Jan Springer

In the land of the rich and famous, Kidnap Fantasies is the answer to discreet naughty downtime.

When ex-downhill skier Jade Hart's two sisters give her a Kidnap Fantasies questionnaire, Jade is aroused at the prospect of having no-strings fun in the sun with a stranger whose only job would be to fulfill her every intimate fantasy. Although she knows she's too shy to send it in, she secretly pours her deepest wishes into the questionnaire. Soon the questionnaire mysteriously vanishes, and Jade's fantasy man appears on her luxury yacht in the form of a sexy handy man who gives her an intimate toy-filled Christmas holiday she'll never forget.

~*~

The Biker and The Bride

Jan Springer

Wrapped in red-hot lust for revenge, Avery plots to murder the man responsible for the death of her son. Her plans are dashed when her ex-husband crashes her wedding and whisks her away on his motorcycle to the rustic Canadian wilderness cabin where they'd once honeymooned.

Police detective Mason is fighting for Avery's love with everything he has.

Armed with whipped cream, handcuffs and his undying devotion, Mason vows he will make Avery love again. But it's only a matter of time before the man she'd planned to kill hunts them down...

~*~

Sinderella Sexy
Jan Springer

By day, she's a dedicated gynecologist.
By night, Dr. Ella Cinder, escapes reality by secretly performing in her own erotic, adult version of Cinderella, aptly retitled Sinderella.
When sexy colleague Dr. Roarke Stephenson shows up in the Sinderella audience on the same night her Prince Charming stands her up, Ella seizes the opportunity to make Roarke into her Prince Charming for one carnal night of extremely naughty fun in front of an audience.

But at the strike of midnight, Ella knows she must face the harsh reality that Roarke must never learn her secret life and they can never be together again. Until then, she'll make sure he'll never forget their night of sensual play.

Dr. Roarke Stephenson is immediately captured by the lusciously curvy actress who hides behind a mask and is known only as Sinderella. For some insane reason, she reminds him of his klutzy co-worker, Ella. But that's not possible. Ella would never have the nerve to do the wickedly delicious things Sinderella does to him...or would she?

~*~

Nice Girl Naughty
Jan Springer

Blind since the age of nineteen, Summer has blossomed into a famous wood carver. When she's almost killed by a serial killer, she's whisked away to a secluded wilderness cabin by the man she once secretly loved.

Summer can't get enough of touching professional bodyguard Nick Cassidy's thick, powerful muscles and all those other hard, yummy male body parts that she has always longed to explore.

For years, Nick has stayed away from his best friend's kid sister, nice girl Summer. Now he's back, and sweeping his gorgeous redhead into the naughty cravings he's always had for her. With passion blinding him, Nick doesn't realize their hideout isn't safe—until it's too late.

Please note: The titles in Naughty Girl Desires have been previously published.

What You'll Find In The
Merry Ménage Kisses Boxed Set
Wrap yourself in four sexy holiday themed adult romance ménages.

A Homecoming Ménage Christmas

Jan Springer

Rachel has a *very* naughty secret and she's way too embarrassed to let anyone know about it. When The Key Club throws a Santa Fetish Ménage Night, it's almost too good to be true. She *has* to figure out how to participate without anyone finding out!

Key Club bartenders Rob and Ron Simpson have fallen head over Santa hats for quiet, nice-girl Rachel. But she has no clue how they feel about her. But she *will* know, because Rachel is coming home from a trip to Europe and the twin brothers are going to give her the best Homecoming Ménage Christmas ever. They'll do it with the help of some naughty toys, the Red Room, a safe word and...Santa Claus.

A Merry Ménage Christmas

Jan Springer

Dr. Kelsie Madison can't remember the last time she's had no-strings sex and that's her clue she's been working way too hard. It's time to unwind at the Key Club by indulging in a yummy Christmas present for herself. Something she's never experienced before — a red-hot ménage.

ER doctor Ryder Greene and his roommate, physiotherapist Dixon Flynn, love sharing their women. They've had their eye on cute Dr. Kelsie Madison for quite some time, but she's a workaholic and she never has time to play.

When they learn she'll be at the Santa Claus Ménage Night festivities, they'll make sure they're the ones kissing Kelsie under the mistletoe. And if they get their wish, Kelsie will be taking them home for Christmas.

Cowboys for Christmas

Jan Springer

Jennifer Jane (JJ) Watson has spent the past ten Christmases in a maximum-security prison.

The last thing she expects is to get early parole, along with a job on a remote Canadian cattle ranch serving Christmas holiday dinners to three of the sexiest cowboys she's ever met!

Rafe, Brady and Dan thought they were getting a couple of male ex-cons to help out around their secluded ranch, but instead they get an attractive and very appealing female.

In the snowbound wilds of Northern Ontario, female companionship is rare.

It's a good thing the three men like to share...

They're dominating, sexy-as-sin and they fill JJ with the hottest ménage fantasies she's ever had. Suddenly she's craving cowboys for Christmas and wishing for something she knows she can never have...a happily ever after.

Christmas Lovers

Jan Springer

Sergeant Connor Jordan, wounded overseas and sent back to the States to recuperate, just cannot stop fantasizing about the sexy nurse who cared for him. When his brothers give him a holiday gift certificate to Kidnap Fantasies, a top-secret fantasy organization, Connor knows he'll use their gift, if only to help him forget his wickedly delicious attraction to Nurse Sparks.

Nurse Tania Sparks has always been purely professional with her injured soldiers...until sinfully sexy Connor Jordan enters her hospital. He makes her body throb with an intense desire she's never known before. The last thing she wants is to get involved with the injured warrior. So what's a woman supposed to do to relieve her naughty frustrations? Call Kidnap Fantasies and have them supply her with a look-alike man who'll help her forget her sexy soldier...

When Tania and Connor unexpectedly come together at a secluded mountain chalet, their love explodes in a ménage of passion, sensuous desires and a happily forever after.

Contains ménage scenes.

Series

The Outlaw Lovers series
2 book bundle
The Outlaw Lovers (includes Jude Outlaw & The Claiming)

A fast-acting virus has killed a majority of the world's female population. Women's rights are stripped away and The Claiming Law is created, allowing groups of men to stake a claim on a female—as their sensual property.
*After five years of fighting in the Terrorist Wars, the Outlaw brothers are coming home to declare ownership on the women they love...and they'll do it any way they can in **Book 1 Jude Outlaw and Book 2 - The Claiming**.*

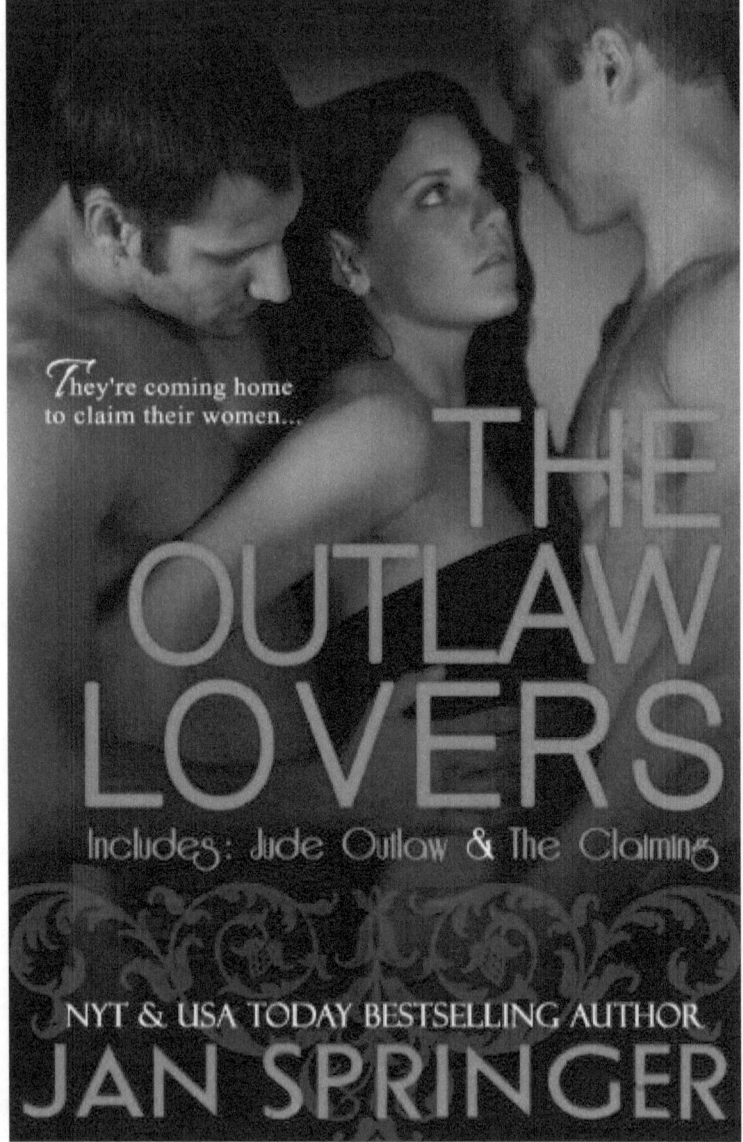

They're coming home
to claim their women...

THE
OUTLAW
LOVERS

Includes: Jude Outlaw & The Claiming

NYT & USA TODAY BESTSELLING AUTHOR
JAN SPRINGER

Jude Outlaw
The Outlaw Lovers 1

When Cate Callahan learns Jude is coming home from the Terrorist Wars and is ready to claim her under the new law—with the help of his four brothers—she steals their boat and escapes to the high seas. Unfortunately, her runaway bid for freedom doesn't last long.

Quickly capturing his lover, Jude rekindles the flames and seduces Cate back into his bed.

But Jude holds a secret that could make him lose Cate forever...

The Claiming
The Outlaw Lovers 2

Seeking refuge from the Claiming Law, Callie Callahan hides in a deserted cabin in the Maine woods and is shocked when her ex-flame finds her. She's always craved being in Luke Outlaw's arms. Tasting him. Touching him. Taking him deeply within her. So, what's a girl to do but to delve into the sinful delights he offers?

Luke has finally reunited with the love of his life. He knows there is only one way to keep Callie safe and with him forever. He'll do it with the help of his three brothers and an assortment of naughty toys. Rekindling the flames between them, he unleashes Callie's sensual side, taking her in ways she never dreamed possible, all with the ultimate goal of presenting her to the Outlaw Lovers and The Claiming.

...wicked desires

COLTER'S REVENGE

The Outlaw Lovers

NYT & USA TODAY BESTSELLING AUTHOR

JAN SPRINGER

Colter's Revenge
The Outlaw Lovers Book 3

A fast-acting virus has killed a majority of the world's female population. Women's rights are stripped away and The Claiming Law is created, allowing groups of men to stake a claim on a female—as their sensual property. After five years of fighting in the Terrorist Wars, the Outlaw brothers are coming home to declare ownership on the women they love...and they'll do it any way they can...

Revenge belongs to Dr. Colter Outlaw when he unexpectedly reunites with the beautiful woman who broke his heart during the Terrorist Wars. Capturing her and collaring her, he seduces her, fills her with wicked desires and naughty cravings for a delicious ménage. Fully intent on breaking her heart and walking away, Colter's plans unravel when he submits to the carnal pleasures Ashley gives him so freely.

Colter had told her he loved her. He'd whispered promises of rescue from her life as a slave, but when he'd suddenly disappeared, she'd been devastated. Infected with a version of the X-virus that leaves Ashley Blakely sexually excited on a daily basis, she has come to Pleasure Palace to bid on a cure for her illness. She never expected her Outlaw Lover to be there and screw her plans. Nor did she expect to give him her heart and body so easily...

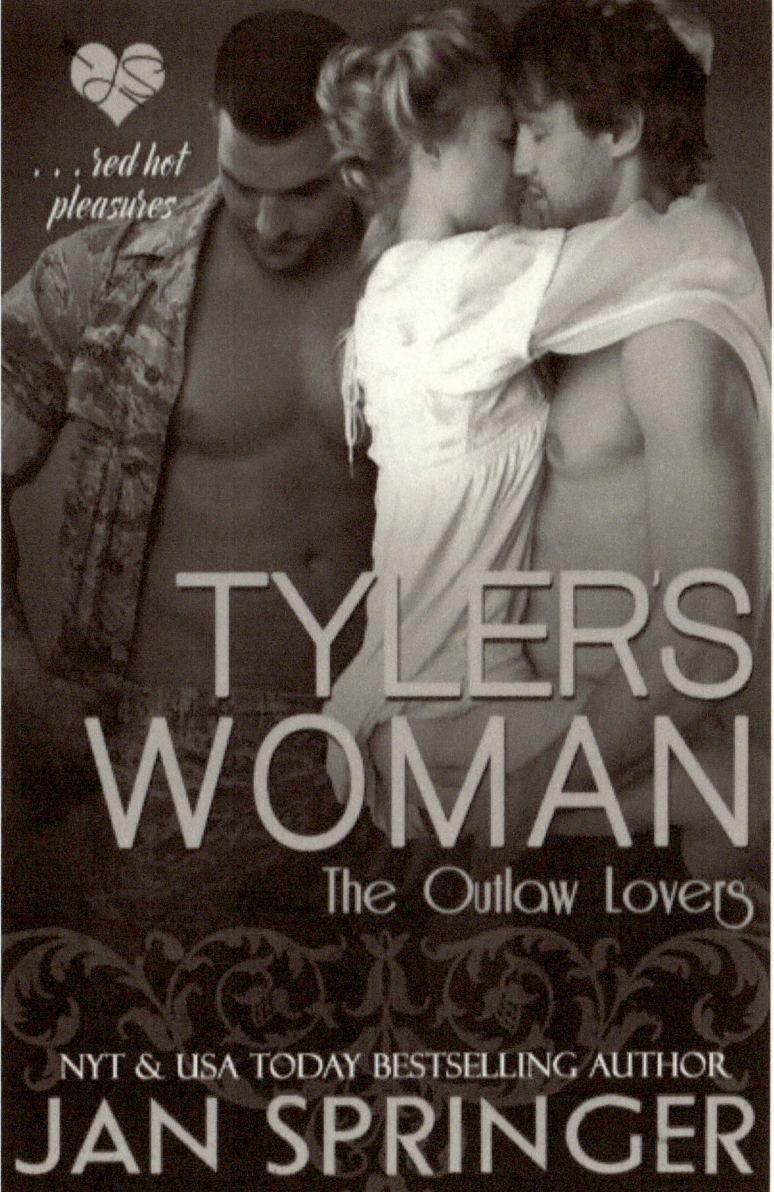

... red hot
pleasures

TYLER'S
WOMAN

The Outlaw Lovers

NYT & USA TODAY BESTSELLING AUTHOR
JAN SPRINGER

Tyler's Woman
The Outlaw Lovers 4

A fast-acting virus has killed a majority of the world's female population. Women's rights are stripped away and The Claiming Law is created, allowing groups of men to stake a claim on a female—as their sensual property. After five years of fighting in the Terrorist Wars, the Outlaw brothers are coming home to declare ownership on the women they love...and they'll do it any way they can...

Laurie Callahan has always experienced red-hot pleasure and passionate love in Tyler Outlaw's arms. But when he's pronounced MIA, presumed dead in the Terrorist Wars, her world is shattered and her heart broken.

For years Tyler Outlaw and his best friend Hunter Brown endured brutal torture and worse in a terrorist prison. Finally free of their hell, they return home intent on seducing Laurie into their erotic-filled fantasies.

Shocked to discover Tyler is alive and he's taken a male lover, Laurie is thrust into a sensual world of sizzling seductions, scorching ménages and the carnal desires that both men crave. But she fears Tyler won't want her when he discovers she's not the same woman he left behind.

...sizzling temptations

RESISTANCE

The Outlaw Lovers

NYT & USA TODAY BESTSELLING AUTHOR

JAN SPRINGER

Resistance

The Outlaw Lovers 5

*A fast-acting virus has killed a majority of the world's female population.
Women's rights are stripped away and The Claiming Law is created,
allowing groups of men to stake a claim on a female—as their sensual
property.*

Fugitive female... Renegade Resistance leader Reena "Red" Wilde is in
for the fight of her life when she experiences an erotic attraction to the
two most dangerous men she's ever met.

Black ops assassin... Months ago, Will "Blade" Smith spent one
sizzling evening in the arms of a red-haired seductress. Now she's his
next assignment. One look into her gorgeous eyes and he's wrestling his
heated cravings all over again.

Bounty Hunter... When Cade Outlaw nabs his bounty, sexy-as-sin
Reena Wilde, his profession dictates she's hands-off. But he can't ignore
the magnetic sparks between them...or that she is the biggest
temptation of his life.

Resistance is futile... After Reena escapes Cade and Will and falls
prey to a band of evil hunters, she's grateful her sexy hunks come to
her rescue, and in return, saves their lives. Trapped in a solitary cabin
during a wicked snowstorm, she can't resist her two well-hung studs,
nor can she deny they've claimed her heart.

...dark
seductions

PLEASURE BURN

The Outlaw Lovers

NYT & USA TODAY BESTSELLING AUTHOR

JAN SPRINGER

Pleasure Burn
The Outlaw Lovers 6

A fast-acting virus has killed a majority of the world's female population. Women's rights are stripped away and The Claiming Law is created, allowing groups of men to stake a claim on a female—as their sensual property.

Suicide Mission...

Mac Outlaw knows that someone needs to take down the dictators that have taken a firm hold on the United States. His best friend, Reece McKenna, has found the perfect way to do it - but it's a suicide mission for all involved. Mac has volunteered...he just didn't expect sexy and stubborn Maggie Wilde, the young woman he can't stand, to be the other volunteer for the mission.

Dark Revenge...

Reece McKenna has dark revenge in his heart and he's willing to do whatever it takes to kill the dictators who have taken everyone he has ever loved. When his best friend along with a tempting, desirable woman offer themselves as the sacrifice to the mission that will end his misery – he knows vengeance will finally belong to him and he won't let anyone or anything stand in his way.

A killing machine...

Maggie Wilde heard that Mac Outlaw and Reece McKenna were just as sweet as a teddy bears. They are anything but after returning from the Terrorist Wars as she quickly learns when she begins training to become a lethal killing machine under the guise of a submissive pleasure slave. Night after night wrapped in their strong arms and sandwiched between their hot bodies, Maggie must fight her growing desires for both men.

Forbidden love...

Passions and pleasures become addictive and forbidden love melts the walls around both men's icy hearts, threatening to destroy a dangerous mission that could set millions of women free of the destructive restraints of the Claiming law.

Kidnap Fantasies Series

In the land of the rich and famous, the top-secret Kidnap Fantasies is the answer to discreet and naughty downtime.

Book One

Jade's Fantasy

When ex-downhill skier Jade's two sisters give her a Kidnap Fantasies questionnaire, Jade is aroused at the prospect of having no-strings fun in the sun with a stranger whose only job would be to fulfill her every intimate fantasy. Although she knows she's too shy to send it in, she secretly pours her deepest wishes into the questionnaire.

Soon the questionnaire mysteriously vanishes and Jade's fantasy man appears on her luxury yacht in the form of a sexy handy man who gives her an intimate toy-filled holiday she'll never forget.

Book Two
Christmas Lovers
(can also be found in the Merry Ménage Kisses Boxed Set)
Sergeant Connor Jordan, wounded overseas and sent back to the
States to recuperate, just cannot stop fantasizing about the sexy nurse
who cared for him. When his brothers give him a holiday gift
certificate to Kidnap Fantasies, a top-secret fantasy organization,
Connor knows he'll use their gift, if only to help him forget his
wickedly delicious attraction to Nurse Sparks.
Nurse Tania Sparks has always been purely professional with her
injured soldiers...until sinfully sexy Connor Jordan enters her hospital.
He makes her body throb with an intense desire she's never known
before. The last thing she wants is to get involved with the injured
warrior. So what's a woman supposed to do to relieve her naughty
frustrations? Call Kidnap Fantasies and have them supply her with a
lookalike man who'll help her forget her sexy soldier...

When Tania and Connor unexpectedly come together at a secluded mountain chalet, their love explodes in a ménage of passion, sensuous desires and a happily forever after.

Contains ménage scenes.

Book Three
Zero to Sexy

Because Santana hides from something bad in his past, he lives only for the moment and doesn't dare dream of a future. He exists within the sensual world of Kidnap Fantasies, a top-secret escort world where he explores his sexuality and enjoys pleasure with both men and women.

But it is love at first sight the instant he sees Amy at his good friend's wedding. She's got future written all over her. He knows she is a hunger he must deny, so why is he whispering "you're mine" to her at the wedding?

The instant Amy Sparks sees the handsome African-American at her sister's wedding, she knows in her heart that he's everything she's ever fantasized about in a lover—but before they can connect, he mysteriously disappears. Upon discovering he works for Kidnap

Fantasies, Amy knows how he'll make all her intimate fantasies come true...

When Santana's next Kidnap Fantasies assignment turns out to be Amy, he knows he must protect her from his past and he can be with her only this one time...

Reader Advisory: Includes a sizzling ménage scene and some male-on-male sensual interaction.

For more Jan Springer stories, please visit http://www.janspringer.com

Jan's Newsletter

Hi! If you would like to get an email when my books are released, you can sign up here:
Newsletter: http://ymlp.com/xguembmugmgb
Your emails will never be shared and you can unsubscribe whenever you like.

Discover Other Titles by Jan Springer
http://www.janspringer.com

~*~

About the Author

Jan Springer writes full-time at her home nestled in cottage country, Ontario, Canada. She enjoys hiking, kayaking, gardening, reading and writing. She is a member of the Writers Union of Canada and the Romance Writers of America. She loves hearing from her readers.

A Word From The Author

Hi! Thank you for purchasing this book. Word of mouth is important for any author to succeed. If you enjoyed this story, feel free to leave a short review at the place where you bought it. I would really appreciate it. I look forward to bringing you more stories in the near future. Thanks!

If you would like to contact me or personally send me feedback, you can reach me by using my contact page at:
http://janspringerauthor.wordpress.com/contact/

Here are other ways we can connect:

Jan Springer Website at http://www.janspringer.com

Facebook - https://www.facebook.com/janspringereroticromance

Twitter - https://twitter.com/janspringer @janspringer

Pinterest - http://www.pinterest.com/janspringer1/

Jan's Blog - http://janspringerauthor.wordpress.com/blog-2/

LinkedIn - http://ca.linkedin.com/in/janspringerauthor/

Google Plus - https://plus.google.com/u/0/
101527334949931513035/posts

Jan's Newsletter - http://ymlp.com/xguembmugmgb

Goodreads - https://www.goodreads.com/author/show/
260628.Jan_Springer

Happy Reading,

Jan Springer

Don't miss out!

Visit the website below and you can sign up to receive emails whenever Jan Springer publishes a new book. There's no charge and no obligation.

https://books2read.com/r/B-A-WGQ-KWNK

BOOKS 2 READ

Connecting independent readers to independent writers.

www.ingramcontent.com/pod-product-compliance
Lightning Source LLC
Chambersburg PA
CBHW030546130626
46552CB00006B/2452